CHRISTMAS STORIES

CHRISTMAS STORIES

7 Original Short Stories

KEVIN MOORE

ISBN: 1522977775
ISBN 13: 9781522977773
Library of Congress Control Number: 2015921497
CreateSpace Independent Publishing Platform
North Charleston, South Carolina

CONTENTS

THE SANTA SUIT

Judge Not, Lest You Be Judged

MATTHEW 7:1

My mother and I hardly ever saw my grandfather, although we only lived forty-five minutes away by car. Mom and Grandpa had had a strained relationship since her childhood, and it had never gotten better; in fact, it appeared to get worse, especially since the recent death of my grandmother. This did not prevent Mom from calling him to ask whether I could stay with him for two weeks. Judging from the tone of her voice, I could tell that the conversation was not going well. My mom and Danny O'Brien, my mother's second husband, were trying to reconcile their relationship. They felt a two-week trip with just the two of them would be a good start.

"I know it's Christmas," my mother said, sounding irritated while on the phone, "but two weeks without me is not going to kill him. Besides, he needs a man in his life, and Danny has been a good father." I had to agree with her to a certain extent—Danny *could* be a real cool guy, but at other times, he was a moody, quiet man, whose buttons my mother could easily push.

"Dad," she said, "if I had anyone else to leave him with, don't you think I would?" Danny, as my mother had told me, was her last chance at a successful relationship. She'd been in many relationships in her past: two marriages and one live-in. The man she had lived with but never married was my biological father and, from all accounts, was "a disaster of a man."

After several minutes, the telephone conversation ended, and she announced that I'd be spending Christmas vacation with my grandfather. I was not overjoyed with that prospect, but I have learned several things in my young life, and one of them is not to cause too many problems, especially where my mother, Jackie, is concerned.

"It's only for two weeks," Mom said, trying hard to reassure me. But this was no comfort—due in part to all the stories Mom had told me about Grandpa over the years.

My grandfather had been in World War II as a young man, and he never went back to Brooklyn, his birthplace. Returning from the Pacific in 1945, at the age of twenty, he settled in the San Fernando Valley, where he met and married my grandmother. They raised my mother and her brother, Joe, in the valley. According to my mom and Uncle Joe, Grandpa did not take much interest in their lives unless my grandmother insisted him to do so. He was Italian, Grandma was Irish, and, according to their children, they used to have some real bouts. I guess they were passionate people—Mom says she yells because she's passionate, and I can tell you that she yells a lot.

Grandma really loved my grandfather, and he loved her, too. I could tell from the way he sobbed at her funeral. He did not cry, however, at Uncle Joe's funeral. Grandpa was strong for Grandma's sake, and he took great care of her during her time of grief. "Emotionless" was the way everyone described Grandpa, and he typically was—except with Grandma. Mom always insinuated that Uncle Joe's drug problem had a lot to do with Grandpa. In fact, she blamed many of her own problems on him.

With that in mind, two weeks seemed an enormous amount of time to spend with him. But my choices were limited. You see, I don't make friends easily, so it wasn't like I had a lot of options. It was different when Grandma was alive—she was warm and friendly and always took great care of me. I had not spent ten minutes alone with Grandpa in the two years since she died.

The small 1940s bungalow where my mother grew up was the same house where Grandpa lived. He and Grandma bought it in 1947, the year they were married, and they never lived anywhere else. I had stayed at Grandpa's one other time in my life, when I was seven. Grandma was still alive then, so I spent all of my time that weekend with her—which was just fine with me.

Mom dropped me off on Friday afternoon, ten days before Christmas. As I pushed opened the gate of the freshly painted, white picket fence that surrounded the house, a memory from that weekend came back to me. It was June, and the three of us—Grandma, Grandpa, and I—had been working in the garden. They had a can of beer each, and I had lemonade. They laughed about something—I don't remember what. Everything was fine until Grandma said how much I looked like Uncle Joe. He had died earlier that year. Grandpa stood up, finished his beer, and went into the house to get a jacket. Then he left and didn't return until very late that night.

"Keep your chin up, boy." My grandfather's voice jerked me back to the present. I looked up to find him standing on the front porch, waiting for me. I straightened up immediately. He'd always commented on my slouch, and I was mad at myself for not hearing him come out of the house. Grandpa had such a big deep voice, but he moved liked a cat. I wished I could put a bell on him.

Mom came up the walk behind me carrying my suitcase, which was a mistake because it gave Grandpa another thing to comment on.

"Boy's ten years old; he should be carrying his own suitcase." I turned to my mother to take the suitcase, but she was not scared of him and ignored what he said. Grandpa patted my head and pecked Mom on the cheek—no hugs for anyone.

All the furniture, pictures, and paintings in the house looked the same as I'd remembered them. I'm guessing it had been like that when my mother was a girl. The only difference was the television in the living room. It was newer. He'd bought it when we were visiting last summer. My mother put the suitcase down in the middle of the living room, and Grandpa told me to take it into my mother's old bedroom.

"You know the rules," Grandpa said, stopping me in my tracks because I did not know the rules. "No drinking and no women."

"I don't know any girls," I said, taking him very seriously. I picked up the suitcase, took it into my mother's old bedroom, and placed it on the bed. Then I said good-bye to Mom, who gave me no instructions. She thanked my grandpa for having me. He nodded, and then Mom was gone, leaving us in the middle of the living room, alone.

The first couple of days together were uneventful. Grandpa asked me what I normally did, because he was "not going to entertain anyone." I watched plenty of television and then cautiously began watching him. Grandpa was definitely a creature of habit. Every morning he got up before 7:00 a.m., made himself coffee and breakfast, and read the paper until about nine. That was about the time I shuffled out of bed.

"There's cereal" would be the first words he greeted me with. While I ate, he would take his morning walk, returning a little over an hour later to sit in front of the television and watch CNN. Then, he would make us both lunch and work on crossword puzzles at the table until about three, when he'd go out for another walk. One afternoon he asked me to come on the walk with him. It was no real mystery. He walked around the neighborhood and apparently knew a good many of his neighbors. When we got home, he'd prepare dinner and watch a little more television. He asked me whether I liked *Jeopardy*. I shrugged. "Well," he said. "If you want, you can pick something tonight. I don't want to hog the TV."

I really didn't know what to make of Grandpa. Sometimes he would try to reach out to me, and sometimes he was just a man of routine. "We can walk and get an ice cream if you want to get out of the house," he offered one night.

"If you want," I replied, not sure whether he really wanted to go for ice cream or was just throwing me a bone.

"I want to know what you want, Matthew."

"Let's watch *Jeopardy*," I said. "We still have doughnuts. I'll get us one."

Grandpa seemed disappointed, but then got up and said "Okay, I'll make some tea."

The next morning, Grandpa surprised me by having breakfast ready for me when I woke up. Scrambled eggs, bacon, orange juice, and pumpernickel toast with grape jelly sat on the table waiting for me. Two plates were set when I walked into the small dining area.

"I'm starving—how about you, kid?" he asked, sitting down and motioning for me to sit.

I ate without saying a word, except to say, "This is very good."

He gave me a slight smile. "You and I need to make a run to the grocery store after you get dressed."

"Okay," I responded. At breakfast, we asked each other some general questions about our lives. Grandpa wanted to know what I ate for breakfast before school and whether Mom cooked.

"Once in a while," I replied. I took a shower while he cleaned up and wrote out a list for the store, and then we were ready to leave.

Grandpa's garage, car, and house all looked like him: clean and in order. He always took a shower early in the morning and put on a clean shirt before starting his day. The Lincoln Town Car was about eight years old, but Grandpa kept it in great shape, and it had only forty-nine thousand miles on the odometer.

"What kind of music do you like, kid?" he asked, as we pulled into Ralphs' Supermarket. I shrugged. I was not sure what I liked, and I was afraid he would think that what I listened to was "crap," which was what Mom called music I listened to occasionally. Before we got started on the shopping list, we went into the deli section, where he had a cup of coffee and I had a cup of tea.

What a difference in shopping styles! Grandpa read every label, but Mom just threw things in the wagon. As we walked past all of the Christmas decorations, I asked him whether he was putting up a tree. "No," he said quickly, his glasses on the edge of his nose. I'd always found Grandpa cold and abrupt, but he surprised me by asking my opinion about most of the foods that he purchased.

After we got back to the house, I noticed a small change in him. He seemed excited as he began pulling out pots and pans, getting ready to cook. "Kid, you want to make a good impression on a woman?" I nodded my head, indicating that I would like that. "I will show you how to make a good Italian gravy, or sauce, that will impress any woman you have over for dinner—guaranteed."

He pulled a stool over to the counter and motioned for me to sit. Then he lined up a variety of items, including red and green peppers, sweet onions, sausage, tomatoes, and fresh basil and rosemary. Never having seen Grandpa cook before, I was surprised by his easy manner, and I joined in eagerly. He showed me how to handle a knife and how to slice the herbs and vegetables with ease. He also explained why each ingredient went into the sauce and how it was needed to enhance the taste.

"Mom uses Ragu," I said, to which he made a face. Later, after he had napped, we set the table and setup for the meal we had planned all day. When he'd served us both, Grandpa poured a Coca-Cola for me and the usual glass of red wine for himself. He had two glasses with dinner. He told me he used to make this dinner for Grandma once a week. That night I found out that Grandpa never dodged a question. If you asked him something, he would answer directly. I was beginning to see Grandpa not as the iceberg I had been brought up to believe he was but as something else entirely.

We now ate all of our meals together. Grandpa would wait for me to wake up in the morning, and we began going out to breakfast every other day. At breakfast, we wouldn't do much talking. Instead, he insisted that I read a piece of the paper, which I did. Sometimes we wouldn't speak for hours, but I began to feel that he was not ignoring me. One day after breakfast, Grandpa asked me whether I missed my mother.

"Yes." He looked at me and asked whether I liked movies. I nodded. "Well, let's go see one this afternoon," he said.

Grandpa didn't talk or eat anything at the movie, but he let me have popcorn and a soda. That night, I thought someone was breaking into the house. First I heard a bang and then I heard a cry—or not really a cry, but something between a cry and a yell. I got out of bed and walked to the hall. It was Grandpa. I could tell he was having a nightmare. I walked to his door but did not enter his room. Standing outside, I heard him calling my grandmother's name, obviously in distress.

"Where's Joe?" he kept saying. "I can't find him." He whimpered like he had been crying, which made me run back to my bed, because I could never ever imagine Grandpa crying. As I lay in bed, I tried to imagine what it must have been like for a child growing up in this house.

The following day, late in the afternoon, Grandpa took me over to Gino's, a small Italian restaurant in Studio City, within walking distance of the house. The place was empty; the staff was busy getting ready for the dinner hour. Grandpa had been quiet all day, much different from the previous few days, and I felt his coldness again. He introduced me to members of the Italian American veterans' group, about eleven men. They were in the final stages of planning an annual Christmas party, which they gave every year for disabled children. After giving me some attention—as well as a Coke—they continued their meeting.

I remembered that Grandpa participated in this event every year. Thinking about how my mother had yelled at him over the phone before I'd left to see him, I now understood that she'd wished he had given her that kind of attention.

The men sat at the table drinking glasses of Chianti and planning the final touches for the party, which was just a few days away. From what I gathered, I could hear their concern about the Santa Claus they had hired this year. They joked about the Santa they had once hired who was so heavy that he broke the chair.

"Thank God he wasn't holding a child," one man chimed in through his laughter.

"You want to look at the toys?" a man asked me. I jumped up and went with him to the storeroom, where they kept the boxes of toys.

On our walk home, I asked Grandpa about the party and why he participated every year. "It's what we do," was all he said.

"Why is Mom always mad at you?" Silence.

We walked at least a couple of blocks before he looked at me and said, "I don't think she thought I was a good father to her or to Joe."

"Did you ever hit them?"

He nodded.

"Mom smacks me." Again, I volunteered information without being asked, and I think Grandpa was surprised.

"Did your mom buy you presents for Christmas?" he asked.

"Money," I replied, without much thought. As we continued walking home, I began to ask him questions that I'd always felt curious about.

"How many kids were in your family, Grandpa? And what were your mother and father like?"

"Eight. Busy with work and kids," were his flat answers.

"Have you ever been lonely, Grandpa?" Approaching a wide street just as the street lights were coming on, he took my hand, and we crossed without waiting for the light to turn green. He did not let go when we reached the other side, and, although I felt awkward, I did not try to pull away.

"Lots of times," he said, finally answering my question. "I'm lonely without your grandma. I'm lonely because I do not understand your mother."

"I meant when you were a kid. Were you lonely then?"

His answer surprised me. He told me that his father had left him at a hospital when he was a child.

"My mother had so many other kids to worry about that she stayed at home. We had no money, so I had to live on a ward with a bunch of other children. My father just dropped me off and left. I think I was six, but I could have been seven. He didn't explain a thing." Grandpa looked at me without emotion and continued. "I think that was the loneliest I've ever felt. I wanted to cry but was afraid that I'd get in trouble." When I reached the gate to the house, Grandpa stopped me. "Why? Do you feel lonely, kid?"

Nodding my head, I said, "Not right now, Grandpa."

In the morning, we went to breakfast at McDonald's. I read the calendar and style sections of the paper, and Grandpa read the front page. I watched his face, but it revealed nothing to me about what he was reading. He looked over the top of the newspaper and stared back at me, raising his eyebrows as if to ask, "What do you want?"

I turned the pages of the newspaper and then looked back down, feigning interest. Sipping his coffee, he put the newspaper down and stared at me. "Do you want to get a Christmas tree?"

"Yes!"

"I haven't had a Christmas tree in two years, so it has to be small," he added, as we got up to go. There were Christmas tree lots all over the valley at this time of year, but Grandpa had a specific place in mind, and that was where we went after breakfast. Not many people were around, so it was a good time to go tree shopping. We browsed through the rows of trees but weren't satisfied with any of the small ones. So we continued our search, and the trees became increasingly larger. After much debate, the one we decided on was bigger than what Grandpa initially intended, but I was very happy with it. It was a beautiful grand fir, about five feet tall, which looked upright and fresh. When he got back to the house, we argued about where to put it.

"We've always put it over there," he said.

"Move the TV. And put the tree closer to the window, so people can see it from the street." I was shocked at my own insistent tone and sudden decision.

"Oh, all right." Grandpa gave in—a total surprise, given his stubborn nature.

Our next job was to find the Christmas decorations, buried somewhere in the back of the garage. He was the supervisor, and I was the labor, but I wanted the decorations more than he did. As we searched, we found several good boxes. These boxes held a lifetime of Christmas memories, and I wanted to put lights and ornaments all around the house. But my biggest surprise was finding a carefully wrapped Santa Claus suit. I took it out of the box, under his protest, and raised the jacket of the suit, looking to him for an explanation. He didn't offer one, so I asked him whom the suit belonged to.

"Me! It's in my house, isn't it?" I was too excited by the Santa suit to be offended by the tone of his voice. I think I was developing the thick skin he had always told me I needed.

"Why do you have a Santa suit?" The bright-red suit, which had been carefully packed, was too much for him to ignore, and he took the jacket from me.

"Your grandmother made me dress up in it for a couple of Christmases when your Mom and Joe were kids." Grandpa as Santa Claus? Mom never mentioned that to me, and it made me wonder whether she remembered.

Saturday came, and Grandpa was nervous about the party for the children's organization, another surprise to me. He entered my bedroom, wanting to inspect what I was wearing to the party.

"You're going to hand out soda, so wear something comfortable." Raising my hands, I let him inspect my jeans and shirt. "You look okay," he said.

We arrived at Gino's early and went into the banquet room to set up for the party. Balloons, tablecloths, and cups were set up as well as a chair for Santa Claus and all the toys he was to hand out to the children. It was a funny sight, watching these tough Italian American veterans running around. All of them were anxious to do their best to throw a good Christmas party for children.

The party almost stopped dead in its tracks when an organizer came running into the room, yelling, "That drunken idiot canceled!"

"Who?" everyone yelled.

"Santa Claus!" What followed was a silence you could have cut with a knife, before the men began asking what happened. Everyone gave his opinion, but it was agreed that the man who was to play Santa was a drunk and should never have been hired.

Someone said, "Now what?" After a brief moment, I spoke up, knowing full well that I would have to pay for it later.

"Grandpa has a Santa suit. He could play Santa Claus." Before my grandfather had a chance to object, we were in a man named Mario's Cadillac on the way back to the house.

There is something to be said about seeing a person out of his or her element, and watching Grandpa dress up as Santa Claus was eye-opening to me. In between his complaints about how he could not pull it off, he stepped into the Santa suit and began to change right before my eyes.

"Get me a pillow, Matthew!" Matthew? Wow, he called me by my name! What happened to "kid"? He turned to face himself in the mirror and asked, "What do you think?" The suit looked good, but the beard was faded and ratty. Somehow, though, it didn't matter; the change was believable.

"You look great, Grandpa. I mean, Santa Claus." Back at Gino's, all of the men had been in a sweat until Mario, Grandpa, and I returned, just as the kids had finished eating. Grandpa walked in to audible sighs of relief, and the kids broke into applause as he strolled to the Santa seat. It was a great day and one Grandpa totally enjoyed. He hugged the children and handed out gifts, "ho-ho-hoing" through it all. Who would have believed that he, of all people, would make a great Santa Claus? Certainly not me, but here it was before my eyes.

Things were slightly different my last few days at Grandpa's. I think both of us were still on a high from the party. We continued to eat all of our meals together, and on Sunday, he made me go to church with him. "You need God in your life, Matthew; don't think otherwise," he said as I grumbled.

On Christmas Eve, the day before my mother came home, Grandpa and I spent the day shopping for a present for her. That night, we made a variety of snacks, so there was no need for a sit-down dinner. We had rented several Christmas films. As Grandpa sat on the couch, I curled up next to him. After a minute, he put his arm around me, and we watched *A Christmas Story*.

Looking back, the Christmas I spent with Grandpa was one of the best I ever had. Mom and Grandpa continued to have their problems, but things got better. I'd often say, "Mom, let it go!" I also insisted we have Grandpa over for Thanksgiving each year. I even talked Mom into helping me take a tree to his house every year, until I was old enough to take one on my own. Still, they were never as big as the first tree we had together. For the remaining Christmases of his life, Grandpa played Santa Claus at the annual Italian American veterans' Christmas party, and he filled the suit better and better each year. Mom did not remember that her father had dressed up as Santa Claus for her and Joe when they were young, and that's okay, because maybe at the time he couldn't fill the suit. It takes a big person with an even bigger heart, and sometimes you have to work into the role. In my eyes, Grandpa did just that. I only hope I can.

The End

COMFORT AND JOY

*What profit is there if you gain the
whole world, but lose your soul?*

MATTHEW 16:26

Margaret O'Hara glided across the decorated lobby of the Plaza Hotel. In her usual detached manner, she admired the Christmas trees carefully placed throughout the lobby and the overhead wreaths lined with lights and colored beads. Maggie, the name she was known by, had that ageless beauty few women possess. She had silky black hair that was rich and full, like her spirit. Her hair fell around her shoulders in a careful style that never looked messy. Maggie's dark hair highlighted a beautiful Irish face and ice-blue eyes, with long, full eyelashes. Soft lines around her eyes and lips gave character to a face that revealed little of the pain she hid from the world or from herself.

She slid out of her cashmere cape as she reached the coat check for Ballroom B. Two law clerks who worked for her firm, Burke, Collins, and O'Hara, were just leaving with coat tickets when she arrived. Music from inside the ballroom spilled into the lobby, like a small wave gently touching the shore. Maggie smiled at the law clerks and said, "The music sounds wonderful." As she handed her coat to the young man at the coat check, she pretended to look in her purse—giving the law clerks time and tactic permission to move away from her.

She looked up at the young man handing her the claim ticket for her coat. He smiled broadly, saying, "Miss, you look beautiful." Maggie liked the idea that she could still attract a young man in his twenties. Vanity, however, was a wasted emotion on her, and she rarely allowed herself to linger there. Maggie's looks always deceived witnesses and opposing attorneys in the courtroom. Others were never quite prepared for her "will of steel"—until it was too late. It was the DA's office that gave her the name "assassin." She wore it proudly in the courtroom because that was the job.

Maggie stood outside the ballroom, where her firm was having its annual Christmas party. Burke, Collins, and O'Hara always gave fabulous parties, which Maggie went along with, not because she enjoyed them but because she considered them good for business morale. Same thing for bonuses.

Taking a deep breath, she looked around at the expensive decorations. She smiled sadly. Christmas was always a hard time of year for her. Sixteen years since the death of Julie and David, and the chains could still be as heavy as ever. Maggie reached for the ballroom door. From the corner of her eye, she caught sight of a woman whose skin looked gray and taut. Before she had a moment to think, she was inside the ballroom, surrounded by celebrants and the sounds of Christmas. Something in the woman's face triggered an unpleasant feeling or memory, neither of which she was willing to explore at that moment. She turned toward the band, which was harmonizing in "Noel," and joined them for a brief moment, singing, "Born is the king of Israel."

Maggie knew her Christmas Party 1996 night would be a carbon copy of last year and the year before that one. First, she would search the crowd for her partners, Bill Collins and Paul Burke, and their wives, Margo and Carol.

Maggie spotted Bill and Margo, and she walked across the ballroom toward the table where the partners were sitting. As she walked by the edge of the dance floor, Paul Burke grabbed her hand and pulled her onto the dance floor. The band played "The Christmas Waltz," and Paul and Maggie gracefully obliged. Paul Burke was like a father or older brother to Maggie, and every year they danced at least twice.

Paul was a good-looking Irishman who loved a few spirits and a good party. Maggie liked Paul with his easy charm.

He had been very good to Maggie after the death of Julie and David. Paul involved her with work, not knowing at the time that she would become the firm's biggest asset. When it came to winning prestigious cases and demanding exorbitant fees, nobody did it better than Maggie O'Hara.

They finished their dance and went to join the others at the table. Stopping a waiter, Maggie took a glass of champagne from his tray. Yes, this Christmas was starting to be more of the same: a few drinks, some social conversation, but no real meaning, no joy for Maggie. She let the champagne lie on her tongue and tingle her lips. Margaret O'Hara had that rare ability to make everyone she spoke to feel like the most important person in the room. She slid through the evening easily enough, with that smile of hers, which carried its own light. She looked beautiful in her blue dress that had just enough sequins to be festive without being flashy.

Everyone around her thought that she was a happy lady because she made each person feel happy. No one knew the emptiness inside that kept her working fourteen-hour days, six days a week. She would walk around her high-priced apartment, looking out at the million-dollar view of New York, and being so removed from her own feelings that she saw nothing but lights, not a city filled with people.

The band began to play a melancholy version of "Have Yourself a Merry Little Christmas." The words and the music touched a place in her heart—a place she thought she had hidden so well that her heart would never dare reveal it. Ah, but the heart does not play fair. Maggie did have moments of personal hope, but for the most part, she had been sleepwalking for the last sixteen years of her life. Yes, she was alive in the courtroom, but her brilliance there could never reach the level of life she had known in a more ordinary setting—a life robbed from her in a few brutal moments. She tried to chase the memory with a sip of champagne.

The emotion she fought mounted quickly as she was flooded with thoughts of Julie. It was so easy for her to see her daughter as she had been all those years ago. That darling little girl, untouched by life—a life filled with the promise that only children can bring. Maggie could remember her vividly, as she came rushing into the kitchen and chanting, "We're going to buy Mommy a present. We're going to buy Mommy a present." Maggie remembered laughing as David came up beside Julie, both of them dressed in coats and scarves. Julie was the picture of David, with her dirty-blond hair, button nose, and brown eyes.

"Well," Maggie said, bending down to kiss her little face for the last time. "Make sure it's a big diamond. You know the kinds of rocks Mommy likes." Julie stepped back, confused by her mother's sense of humor. "No, Daddy said a bike." David and Maggie laughed, and then she—they—were gone.

"Maggie, one drink at JD's?" Bill Collins asked as everyone at the table got ready to leave. The band had stopped playing. Back in the present, Maggie looked at the faces around her, wanting just a few more minutes of her past.

They all filed into JD's, a place they knew well, as they had for the last five years. This fancy New York pub catered to an upscale crowd, and the owner was a client of their firm. Grabbing seats at the bar, several ladies sat, Maggie included. Maggie was the only woman who knew the bartender by name, and she called him over.

"Hi, Miss O'Hara."

"Bob, I would like some comfort because I don't think I'm going to find much joy this season. So if you would be kind enough to open a bottle of Moët and pour me a glass, I will see to it that the bill gets paid and that Bill gives you more than a ten percent tip."

Bill laughed. "Dear girl, you are the one with the suitcases filled with money."

"I knew the mention of money would get your attention," Maggie said. They all laughed at Bill's legendary tightfisted reputation.

Maggie sat sipping her champagne and trying hard to remember the title of the Christmas carol playing over the pub's expensive stereo system. Memory was ironic at times. Julie had always been accessible to Maggie, and she could remember details of her daughter's short life, no matter how painful they were. It could have been two weeks ago since the accident; that was how fresh Maggie's pain felt. Thoughts of Julie drifted to thoughts of David, the time when she began to understand that he was not exactly the man he pretended to be. When she'd met him, he had already been married and divorced, and had a little girl named Debbie.

After several years of marriage, Maggie began to see that David always presented himself as the victim, and she became disappointed with him. He claimed that his divorce was not his fault. The fact that he saw his daughter only a few times a year was not his fault, losing his job—not his fault. Maggie realized that David had a way of pretending to be something he was not. Inevitably, his failure to take responsibility would be exposed. He then would make it someone else's problem and move on like an observer, not like the catalyst he was.

Still, as smart as Maggie was, she never knew for sure whether he'd had extramarital affairs. Months after his death, she discovered from family and friends that David had had two affairs. Everyone thought she'd be devastated by this news, but she wasn't, since David was no longer capable of hurting her, and she had not been in love with him for years. Julie was more important to her than a marriage with bells and whistles. All in all, she had loved David. They'd always made each other laugh, which had been enough to keep the marriage going.

At the time, Maggie overlooked the fact that he was weak, although she was tired of being his mommy. If she had known of the affairs, she would have divorced him. However, she never tried to catch him in the act. Maggie didn't use private detectives the way she did now when working on a case. In all honesty, Maggie did not mourn the loss of David the way she thought she should. Julie was the one she was never able to get over. Her life would never be normal again. Maggie tried hard to lock all the windows and doors to her emotions.

Everyone was laughing and having a good time when Maggie said her good-byes and slipped away. The wind blew her hair gently around her face when she stepped out of JD's. As she looked for a taxi, she realized she'd had too much champagne. A cab pulled in front of the pub and she gracefully got in. She looked out the window at the lights that decorated the city. New York was the best-dressed city in the world at Christmastime.

Thoughts of Julie and her annual Christmas trip into the city filled Maggie's mind. They would rent a room for the night, take Julie to Radio City Music Hall, have a ride in a carriage through Central Park, and, of course, visit Santa Claus at Macy's. Maggie so enjoyed being a mother that she left her law practice when Julie was two to become a full-time mom; it was the happiest time of her life.

The cab traveled a few blocks before Maggie realized the cab driver had been watching her through the rearview mirror. She looked out the window, trying hard to separate herself from the world of Christmas, but she could not escape Christmases past. The poor lady was in constant battle: She wanted to chase some of the memories away, but they were all she had left, and any memory was better than no memory.

"Julie, Julie, do you love me? Julie, Julie, Julie, do you care?" Maggie moved uncomfortably in her skin as the old Bobby Sherman song played in her head. She would always sing this song to her daughter, and Julie would always come into the room yelling, "Yes, Mommy, yes!"

Tears began to run down her face and quickly turned into sobs. After a brief moment, the cabbie spoke. "The party could not have been that bad." Maggie looked up, surprised that he had broken into her private thoughts, and laughed.

"Oh no?" she said, wiping her eyes.

"You know, it's natural to mourn the loss of someone we love, but you must find something to live for again. Otherwise, the only thing we have from that life is sadness—nothing of the joy or what we learned from them." That was what her therapist said years ago when she used to see her on a once-a-week basis, but she stopped. Not enough time.

Maggie stared out the window at a homeless man in the cold pushing a grocery cart.

For sixteen years, she was emotionally crippled. While her career took off like a rocket, her spiritual and emotional life was like a train stuck at the station—she was never able to get started again. This was the time of year she was the most vulnerable. Her wounds were always scratched, and then they'd open with the memory of Julie. Her soul was trapped. Maggie had tried everything, or at least that's what she told herself—a therapist, expensive trips, yoga, church, and jogging. She dated. One guy even asked her to marry him, but she felt nothing like that for him and immediately broke it off.

She went over that day again in her mind, replaying the last minutes of her time with Julie. Julie sitting in the front seat, waving good-bye as snowflakes fell. Maggie was watching from the porch of her Yonkers home, preparing to go inside and wrap all the Christmas gifts. December 23 was a date branded into her life because of a drunk driver and bad timing.

Maggie was never able to sell her Yonkers home. Presently, she was still renting the house to an older couple and occasionally found herself parked out in front, especially at this time of the year. Maggie looked at the driver who was babbling about the holidays. She thought of her little house in Yonkers, how beautiful she had kept it when they lived there. There was always something cooking, making the house smell wonderful. She would paint with the little girl and do all kinds of fun projects, which kept her little imagination active. God, how she wanted to blame David. That would have been easier, but she and David had both planned the day and the police said it was the other driver's fault. After all these years, she still longed for a letup in her pain.

"You can't sleepwalk through Christmas—not in this city," the driver said, intruding on her thoughts again.

"Sleepwalk?" she asked.

"It's Christmas. Touch someone, love someone who needs you, and you may find what you need in the bargain." The cab stopped in front of her West Side co-op; the doorman rushed out to open her door.

Stepping out of the taxicab, she wondered to herself, *Who the hell is this guy, and how did he dare to know what I feel? Sleepwalk?* Tell that to the twenty million I've billed this year and the front page of the *New York Times*.

Maggie was up and dressed the next morning early. She had slept solidly and felt great physically. She poured a cup of hickory nut coffee and looked around the spotless apartment. Many cleaning women had come and gone during the years, but eventually she'd let them all go because no one could clean the apartment like her. She filled her life so she had no time to think. After her eighty-four-hour workweek, Maggie cleaned the apartment from top to bottom on Sunday morning.

Her apartment was devoid of Christmas except for the pile of cards she left on the counter and the lovely flowers she always got from the Burkes. All other gifts she received from clients and friends were always passed out to people at work, the doorman, and anyone else who worked in the building, along with cash. Maggie's assistant sent her Christmas cards out, so she was never involved with the season personally.

While she swallowed her last bit of coffee, she called the doorman and asked him to get her a cab. He held the door for her as she hurried out the door of the building and walked into the glare of a sick-looking woman.

Before the young woman could stop her, Maggie was in the cab and on the way to the office. Maggie knew the face belonged to the same woman from the party the night before, but she remembered her from somewhere else. But where? The cab driver this morning was not talkative, which was just as well. Maggie was thinking about the Granger murder. Did she really want to defend Nick Granger?

She walked past her assistant, Janet Jones, and exchanged good mornings, knowing very well that Janet would be in her office shortly, as she had been every morning during the last ten years. Maggie had a large corner office with magnificent views of the city that equaled the views from her plush apartment. The office was filled with antique furniture she had accumulated over the years in places like London and New Orleans.

Nick Granger's file sat in the middle of the oak desk in front of her, and after a few minutes, she finally picked it up. What was it about this case? Why was she having enormous trepidation about handling it? Maggie could not put her finger on it exactly. She gave herself the usual arguments: Maggie, you're a defense attorney—"innocent until proven guilty," the battle cry of defense attorneys everywhere. This was the first case in many years that her gut was telling her not to take. Nick Granger was an extremely wealthy real estate man with a reputation for the ladies. Problem was, Nick was married, although it did not appear to bother him, or Lisa, his wife. After years of knowing of his affairs, Lisa stayed in the marriage and apparently was a very happy woman. That was until a week ago, when she was found dead in her nightly bubble bath.

Reaching for her telephone, Maggie buzzed Paul Burke's extension and asked him to come into her office. Bill Collins had yet to arrive and would have to miss her decision. Paul entered within minutes, carrying a small pot of tea and two cups, leaving the door open. He immediately made himself comfortable on the couch.

"I don't want to defend Nick Granger," she said, waiting for an argument. Bill was not happy she was not taking the case. "Nick Granger is a louse, a liar, a thief, and, some people think, a murderer, but he's entitled to his day in court," he said, taking a sip of tea and wishing Bill had been here to help him try to talk her into defending this high-profile and enormously profitable case. The business side of this case was not lost on Maggie, and as a team player, she had come up with an idea.

"Maybe we can give this to Tom and Ellen. I think they've proven themselves." The Granger case was already all over the tabloids and would become a media frenzy that was watched all over the world.

Paul shook his head. "You're right, they are good, but they're no Margaret O'Hara, and Nick Granger wants you and only you." Maggie raised her hands to the sky, as if to say, "I'm sorry."

Outside of her office, she heard the raised voices of two women. Paul and Maggie's attention went to the door, as Janet approached. Janet, who had a flare for the dramatic, raised her voice higher. "No one sees Miss O'Hara without an appointment."

Maggie caught a glimpse of the woman, the one she had seen earlier in the day.

"It's okay, Janet," Maggie said, as she walked to the door. Like a wave of heat one feels when stepping out of an air-conditioned room into the blazing sun, anxiety hit Maggie. She stared at the stringy-haired woman with the skeleton physique, and a memory came into focus.

Janet stepped out of the way, as the woman carefully walked into the office. "Debbie?" Maggie said with a gasp. The young woman fell against the wall in hopes of some support. "Oh my God!" Maggie took a quick inventory of the woman's condition. Her body was lost in the clothing she wore. The shirt and pants hung on her body as if on a chair. Maggie and Paul helped the woman to the couch as Janet poured her a glass of water.

Maggie sat close to Debbie on the couch. "This is David's daughter from his first marriage, Debbie—Debbie Burns," Maggie told her partners and Janet. Several weeks a year, Debbie had come to Yonkers to stay with her and David. Maggie worried constantly about Debbie's influence on the younger Julie. Debbie always talked back to David, and she and Julie did things that Julie would never think of doing on her own. Thinking of the little girl with the stringy hair, who would stare at her when she thought that Maggie was unaware, made her sad. Maggie had always felt sorry for

Debbie, a child who had always seemed angry and uncomfortable—with herself and with life.

Now this grown woman next to her, with the same confused look in her eyes, looked like she had anorexia. Paul stood to leave, but Maggie motioned for him to stay.

Maggie turned to speak, but Debbie beat her to it. "I'm sorry to bother you. I know you're a big, fancy lawyer." Oh, this is about money, Maggie thought, but Debbie continued. "I need to find someone to adopt my baby, and I thought you could help me, being a lawyer and all. I mean, you must have good clients—do you maybe have one who wants a kid?"

Debbie's face had the expression of a deer caught in a trap. Maggie laughed, not at the young woman, but at herself. "We're defense attorneys. We don't deal with adoption."

The young woman, who was obviously in physical pain, began to cry. "I'm sick," she said with her head down.

"I can see that," Maggie replied. "What's wrong?" Debbie never looked up but spoke between her tears.

"AIDS." Paul decided that this was much too personal a subject and left the office. Maggie stood and walked to her desk.

Debbie tried to control her emotions. "I've been in and out of the hospital over the last year. I've been a bad mother, and I need to make sure she isn't given to the state." She sat alone on the couch, crying.

She looked at the young woman whose life might soon be over. It brought back thoughts of Debbie as a little girl, crying at her father's funeral. It sent Maggie rushing back to the couch, with the ignorance and fear of someone living in 1996. Putting her arms on the girl she had known so many years before, Maggie fought the impulse of her profession. She wanted to ask how she had gotten the disease, but she realized it did not matter. It was obvious to Maggie that she was in the final stages of the disease.

"Who's taking care of your little girl?"

Debbie did not look up when she spoke. "A friend, but she has the virus, so I can't count on her." Maggie began to stroke her hair gently.

Debbie always needed a ribbon or a beret, and Maggie always did her hair nicely when she came to stay with them.

"Where is your mom?"

"She died two years ago when I was pregnant with Lily."

Maggie took a deep breath and asked gently, "Does your daughter have the virus?" Debbie looked up for the first time and shook her head "no."

"I have her tested every few months. I guess that will matter to the people who adopt her." Maggie nodded.

After she had taken her address and called a lawyer friend who handled difficult adoptions, Maggie put Debbie into a cab. She gave Debbie one hundred dollars in the elevator for cab fare and whatever else she needed.

Maggie needed a drink, although it was only eleven in the morning. What a morning, Maggie thought, as she walked the short distance to JD's. She had never expected to see Debbie again, and she was crushed to see that her life might end with this kind of pain. Maggie rubbed her hand, trying to forget the feel of Debbie's bones. The young woman had the body of a holocaust survivor, and it made Maggie feel she had icicles flowing through her own veins.

JD's was just getting ready for the lunch trade when Maggie stepped in. She headed right for the bar, looking very businesslike in her $800 Dior suit. She put her purse on the stool next to her just as the portable telephone rang. Maggie reached into her purse for the telephone as the barmaid arrived. The woman knew Maggie, but Maggie could not recall her name.

"Please hold," she said and then rested the telephone on her lap. Maggie smiled at the woman. "First things first. Glenlivet neat, coffee black." The barmaid went about her business and Maggie took the call: "Maggie." There was a pause as she listened to Janet on the other end of the telephone. "Okay, Granger, six o'clock at the office."

The barmaid put the scotch down in front of her. Maggie picked up her drink and took a long sip. Come on, Maggie; rise to the occasion she thought to herself. Her telephone rang again and Maggie shut it off and put it back into her purse without answering the call.

Donny Jones walked up to the bar and sat next to Maggie. He was a well-dressed man in his late thirties, with supposed Mafia ties. She watched him from the corner of her eye. She was much too involved with her own thoughts to entertain the idea of a conversation.

"Hi, Miss O'Hara, I'm Donny Jones, Nick Granger's personal attorney."

Maggie finished her scotch and motioned to the barmaid for another one. "Hello." Maggie was sorry she'd shut off the telephone, and she checked her watch for effect.

"Nick is worried the DA is going to pick him up in the next couple of days and actually charge him with the murder," Jones said.

Maggie took a drink of her scotch before answering. "Why is he surprised? Isn't that the reason he wants to hire a defense attorney?"

Donny ordered a beer and then turned his attention back to Maggie. "He's not looking for a defense attorney. He has you."

Maggie stood. She'd barely touched her second scotch, deciding that Nick Granger was not the person she wanted to think about or talk to. "I don't talk about potential clients with anyone, except the potential client. I've got to run, Mr. Jones." She put down two twenty-dollar bills and headed for the door, leaving Donny Jones at the bar with the words "potential client" dancing in his head.

Maggie did not like men like Nick Granger and Donny Jones. They were handsome men with plenty of money, who dressed in fancy clothes and lived in high style, but underneath they were dog shit. All the cologne in the world could not hide the smell. Starting to walk back to her office, Maggie changed her mind and walked over to St. Michael's church. She decided to light a candle for Debbie and her daughter, with the hope that God would find the little girl a good home.

Twelve o'clock Mass was underway, and Maggie was surprised; it had been a long time between her attendances at Mass, and she forgot that during the Christmas season there was an afternoon service. She sat at the end of the pew and listened to the priest, who was finishing a reading from the Gospels. He began to talk about the Christmas season and how it was a good time to heal old relationships—relationships with people in our pasts and presents, so we could ease gently into our future relationships. He also talked of healing our relationship with the Lord, especially during this season. Maggie sat, remembering how important her faith had been to her and how she'd always loved telling Julie the story of the birth of Christ. She felt he was speaking directly to her. He ended with, "with God, all things are possible."

Maggie left the church and went to look for a taxi. A cab pulled over and she got in. She reached for her telephone, starting to dial a number as she verbally gave the taxi driver an address.

"You want to go to Yonkers?" the man asked, starting to pull over to let her out.

"There is a fifty percent tip in it for you."

The cab driver looked her over in the rearview mirror and turned the cab back into the traffic. "Hey, I know you. You're that female attorney who kicks ass in the courtroom. So I know you'll make good on the fare."

She smiled at him and then sat back in the seat, struggling to take her coat off with one hand while holding her phone with the other. "Pauline, please. Tell her it's Maggie O'Hara." She looked out the window as she waited for Pauline Turner, with whom she went to law school. Maggie never enjoyed this ride to Yonkers, but today was different; it felt good to get out of the office, away from the pressure of the Granger case.

"Pauline, I need to ask some questions I didn't have a chance to ask this morning. What is the degree of difficulty when it comes to adopting a child with the potential of testing positive?" Maggie was silent for a very long time as she listened. The cab driver listened to his talk show on the radio, not paying any attention to her telephone conversation. Maggie and Pauline exchanged ideas for twenty minutes, but at Pauline's reply, Maggie felt her hopes fade. "Do everything you can."

Maggie closed her eyes. When she opened them, they were outside her Yonkers house. It looked so ordinary in comparison to her memory of it. At first, she always assumed that the tenants were not taking care of it, so she'd hired a man who came around once each quarter. Eventually, Maggie realized that it was her life in this house that kept the property special. In actuality, the house was a small cottage that was seventy-five years old. Maggie stepped out of the cab and walked in front of the house. For the first time in sixteen years, she realized she needed to sell it.

Riding back to New York was a blur. Maggie knew that Debbie would never live to see her daughter placed, and, according to Pauline, there was a "possibility it would never happen." Maggie had to stay positive and had to believe that with all her connections, she would make it work.

The cab stopped in the alley of a run-down tenement building, where fire escapes ran down the back of the building like the spine of a dinosaur. She rummaged through the Christmas envelopes in her purse, where she had inserted Christmas cash for various people who worked for her in some capacity. She took out the money to pay the cab driver, giving him $200 dollars for a one-hundred-dollar fare. Inside, the building smelled of urine, and graffiti plastered the walls. My God! Maggie thought. What a horrible place to raise children.

Climbing several flights of stairs to the third floor, she passed a teenage girl who was smoking a joint. Maggie started to knock on the door of 3C, when a heavyset woman came through the open door across the hall. "Ambulance just took her away."

"Where did they take her?" Maggie asked, fearing the worst.

"Bellevue."

Maggie ran down the stairs, fighting tears. Outside, the street was alive, still going about its daily business. A woman was fighting for her last bit of life, but the world kept turning. She headed toward First Avenue and hailed a cab. Maggie got out at the emergency entrance at Bellevue. Her phone was blowing up: first Janet, and then Paul, and then Bill, and then Granger's secretary.

Maggie went through the emergency room and found out that Debbie had been moved upstairs. She stepped out of the elevator and at the far end of the hall saw a little girl talking to a nurse. Maggie instantly thought it must be Lily, Debbie's child. Lily resembled Debbie as a child: very thin, with straggly hair. She was maybe about two years of age. Maggie strode down the hall, squatted, and started to talk to the child. After a moment, she lifted the little girl and gave her a big hug. The nurse gave Maggie Debbie's dire prognosis. The little girl did not realize the severity of the situation and Maggie wanted to make her happy, so she let her play with her bracelet, which Lily kept touching. Maggie asked the nurse to stay with her for a minute as she walked into the ward to see Debbie.

Debbie looked worse than she had that morning. An oxygen mask covered her mouth, and the doctor was giving the nurse orders.

Maggie walked to the bed and picked up Debbie's hand, holding it gently. "Hi, Debbie, it's Maggie." She looked questioningly up at the doctor, who nodded to reassure her that Debbie could hear her.

"She can hear everything going on in the room," he said with a calming voice Leaning down toward her, Maggie spoke softly. "Everything is going well; I don't want you to worry about Lily. I am taking care of all that..." Maggie wanted to break down and cry, but she knew there would be time for that. For now, she had to reassure Debbie. "I don't want you to be afraid. Your dad, your mom, and Julie will be waiting for you. I will make sure Lily has a good life." Maggie gently stroked Debbie's hair.

After a few minutes, she motioned for the doctor to come out to the hall with her. He told her Debbie had collapsed and that someone had called 911, but when the ambulance got there, only the little girl was in the apartment with her. Maggie asked how much time she had left.

"Not a lot."

She stood, numb. Lily trotted over to her and raised her arms to be picked up, which Maggie did. The two of them hugged tightly, and Maggie began to take charge of the remaining days of Debbie's life.

Before leaving to get back to the office and the Nick Granger affair, Maggie went back into Debbie's room. "Lily will be with me until I find something more suitable—and I will. Do not worry!"

Lily and Maggie walked out of the hospital. She explained to the child that she would be staying with her for a little while. Maggie could not let her go back to that horrible building, and the thought of her being left alone scared the hell out of her.

"Are you hungry? Do you need a diaper change?" Lily shook her head as Maggie went down the list of basics. Tomorrow she would have Janet call state services, foundations, and any other organization to find a home for Lily, or at least some help.

Maggie entered the outer office of Burke, Collins, and O'Hara, holding Lily's hand and carrying a bag of essentials, which included diapers. Except for Collins, Burke, and Janet, the remainder of the staff had gone home.

Nick Granger and her partners had been waiting for quite a while, and men like Nick Granger were not accustomed to waiting for anyone. Maggie sat Lily on the couch with a snack and motioned for Janet to sit with her.

"I won't be long," she said, kissing Lily on her cheek. "I promise." How many promises had been broken? Maggie wondered as she walked into her office.

After a couple of minutes of brief conversation, Maggie switched on her desktop recorder. Nick turned on the charm for her, hoping he could change her mind. Finally, he asked whether he could speak to her alone, which she agreed was fine. Burke and Collins left her office.

Nick was like a big child. At first, he talked sweetly, and then he pleaded. "I thought we had an agreement. I put all my eggs in your basket, and now you pull this crap!" He began to yell and to bully, which Maggie allowed for exactly five minutes, timing it on her watch.

Finally, she stood up from behind her desk. "Lower your voice; there is a child out there whom you will frighten!"

But Nick did not miss a beat, and he kept it coming. "I don't give a rat's ass about that child…this is my life…"

She tuned out the rest of his rant. At that moment, only a woman dying of AIDS in a ward in Bellevue cared what happened to that child. With a flash of realization, Maggie knew that she cared, too. And she knew what she had to do.

Maggie buzzed Janet on her telephone. "Get security, and tell Bill and Paul this meeting is over." She then turned her attention to Nick Granger. "There are plenty of good attorneys in this office and in this city. We can refer you to one, or not. Your money can buy most anything, Mr. Granger, but it cannot buy me."

Bill and Paul walked into her office just as Nick Granger was yelling, "Bitch!" She waited a moment hoping he would regain his composure. "Nick, as you know, from our first meeting and the waiver you signed, I tape all of my meetings. Good luck." Maggie took her purse from the desk and left the office, as Bill Collins and Paul Burke began to console and quiet Nick Granger.

Lily's hand was small and soft, and Maggie held it tightly while she looked for a taxi. They chatted and walked until a cab pulled to the curb. Inside the cab, she called the hospital to check on Debbie. There was no change. The cab was passing the Plaza Hotel when she instructed "the driver" to stop. Maggie and Lily got out and ran toward the horse and buggies. The moment Nick Granger had said, "I don't give a rat's ass about that kid," Maggie knew that she would adopt Lily. Somebody had to care, and why not her? She had plenty of money and, more importantly, she had plenty of love to give. Maggie knew she needed Lily almost as much as Lily needed her. They climbed into the buggy, while Maggie pointed out lights and points of interest. It would not be easy. Maggie had to bury Debbie, alone, explain to the child what happened to her mommy, and eventually give up the law practice she loved so much. She would stay at home with Lily while she was young, when Lily needed Maggie. Of course, in those early days, there would be many a sleepless night, worrying about Lily testing positive.

Lily never would test positive for HIV, but Maggie did not know that then, nor would she for several years—not until the medical knowledge of HIV and AIDS grew. With all they had to face—the pain and the sorrow— they would have enough love for each other and for the rest of the world. That alone was a miracle. Maggie was no longer a sleepwalker. She was a woman who had come back to life, and, because she did, Lily would grow up with the chance of a sweet life filled with hope and joy.

The End

OH, CHRISTMAS TREE

"There are few symbols in life that can take us through the looking glass, linking our past with the present; the Christmas Tree is one such symbol."

The bright, ruby-red Christmas ornament with the sparkling-white, Santa Claus face caught Bobby Taylor's attention and lured him into the airport lounge. Looking around the bar area, he thought that the tree seemed out of place in the smoke-filled cocktail lounge, where Christmas travelers crowded the bar, preparing for reunions. Gently, he slid his hand around the ornament and lifted it off the tree. Its body was much stronger than it looked, and Bobby cupped the bulb, like he did when he was a child. *Amazing*, he thought, how the right amount of lights and decorations could make everything appear so glamorous and expensive. He stood in the middle of the crowded airport lounge and held the ornament tightly. A little more pressure and he could easily shatter it in his hands.

"I'm dreaming of a white Christmas" filled the air with the familiar ring of Bing Crosby's voice, as travelers walked past him. For a brief moment Bobby felt like he was about to faint. His head started spinning, and the voices around him drifted away. He felt like he was floating in the air and realized that he was actually above his physical body. I must be having a heart attack, he thought to himself, as he looked at his body standing below, dressed in a pair of blue jeans and a red-and-black flannel shirt. A black scarf hung loosely around his neck. *I'm dying. I'm having an out-of-body experience*, Bobby thought, as he began to float higher and higher toward the airport ceiling.

Suddenly, Bobby was standing in the living room of the small New Jersey house that his family rented when he was a child. Lights from the artificial Christmas tree danced on the walls in the tiny living room. Kneeling in front of the tree, he looked at the tags on top of the wrapped gifts for one that had his name, while his mother, older brother, and older sister slept. Sounds of the wind brushing against the house, rattling the windows, made him think of Santa Claus. If Santa Claus were real, he imagined that his sleigh would sound like that when it landed on the roof.

At eight years old, he was not expected to understand all that happened during the past week, but he did. Bobby heard his aunts and grandmother say, "The poor dear never knew his father." His father had been career military, and the consensus was that Bobby was young enough to recover quickly. They were all worried about his older brother, Jim, who "needed a strong hand." Bobby knew right away that the large present was the Pretzel Getzel machine that he had written down on his Christmas list, and his heart skipped a beat, as he ripped into the green-candy-cane wrapping paper. His mouth watered at the thought of all the delicious pretzels to come. Peggy, his older sister, had gotten an Easy-Bake Oven several Christmases past, but he had not been allowed to use it because "it was for girls."

Looking around the room, he felt a chill. He pulled his bathrobe closed and thought about how different Christmas was this year. News that his father had been killed in Vietnam had come a couple of days ago, the morning of the Christmas pageant. His family had been sitting down to breakfast when a strange man showed up at the door with Mr. Miller, who was a member of the local VFW. No one else seemed to know where Vietnam was, but Bobby did.

One night, after they had received a letter from his father, his mom told him his dad was off fighting a war in Vietnam.

"Where's that?" Bobby had asked.

"A world away," Mom said. So Bobby went to the library the next day and asked the librarian the same question. She showed him Vietnam on a map. Mom was right: It was a world away.

A long, thin package with his name on it caught his eye, and Bobby reached over and picked it up. "Love, Peggy" was written on the small card attached to the gift. Peggy was his older sister, and she always gave fun gifts. Bobby was sure it had to be a kite. Holding the gift in his hands took him instantly back to how frightened he was at the sound of his mother screaming in response to the news, the shrillness of her screaming inescapable.

Crying and screaming—that was all anyone had been doing during the past three days. Everyone kept saying that Bobby had never had a chance to know his father, because he was in the military and had been gone most of the last five years. But that was not true. Bobby did know him. He was the smiling man in all the pictures they had around the house.

Bobby put the gift back under the tree and reached for a larger present. He squealed with delight as he ripped through the wrapping paper. Ah ha! It was, it had to be, Tricky Tommy Turtle! Bobby sat for a moment with the joy of the gift. "Dad had the greatest laugh," Mom would always say, when Bobby asked what his father was like. He looked at Tricky Tommy Turtle, and then at all the pictures of his father that had been set out on the end table. The smiling man smiled, as Bobby sat in front of the blinking Christmas tree and slowly began to cry.

Christmas had been a long time coming. Now everything was different, and he knew that it would never again be the same. Looking away from the pictures, Bobby turned his attention to the blinking Christmas lights. He reached over, cupped his hands around a red, blinking light, and watched them glow with illumination. He wanted so much to capture the magic of the lights and the way they made him feel.

Bobby closed his eyes for a moment and wished fervently that it were last Christmas. He let go of the light, and his small hand brushed gently against the bright-red ornament with the sparkling-white Santa Claus face. His father had hung the very same Santa Claus face ornament on the "real" Christmas tree just the year before, as opposed to the fake one Mom put up this year and that was something Bobby did remember about his dad.

"Why isn't there a Santa Claus? Why?" he repeated aloud to himself. Slowly, Bobby reached for the ornament, took it off the tree, and held it in his hands. "Why? Why did you have to die, Daddy?" He looked down at the ornament as he squeezed it tighter and tighter until it shattered.

Suddenly, Bobby found himself back in the airport lounge—the bright-red ornament with the sparkling-white Santa Claus face, in fragments in his hands. He stared at the broken glass, relieved that there was no blood. Bobby glanced around desperately missing his young son. He hurried to a trash can to brush the glass from his hands, and then he turned and headed for the plane home.

Adelyne stirred her coffee in a complete circle while slowly pouring "natural, raw" sugar into the cup. She glanced at the clock behind the coffee counter in Starbucks and then checked the gold Citizen watch on her arm to confirm the time. She had two hours until the plane landed—plenty of time for a small adventure. She took a sip of the seven-bean, house-blend coffee and decided to walk around the airport and people-watch.

Another sip of coffee, and Adelyne got off the stool and straightened the navy-blue sport jacket she was wearing over a white turtleneck shirt. She took her coffee over to the trash can and poured a little out into the garbage. There, she thought, that will make it easier to walk around the airport.

Age had been kind to Adelyne, both physically and mentally. It had also allowed her to be truthful with herself. Nothing she did was without careful planning and meticulous timing, on even the simplest of tasks.

Christmas travelers rushed past her as she stepped out of Starbucks. Most had the crazed look in their eyes that many people get at this time of year—so much to do and not enough time to do it all. Adelyne was well aware that her careful planning and organization skills could annoy people. Hell, it drove the love of her life, Harry, crazy for forty years. She laughed aloud at the thought. A family of four came running past her, obviously late for their plane. Adelyne saw strain on the woman's face; she seemed to be suppressing a need to tell the rest of them that the trip was entirely too much work.

Watching them, Adelyne decided to play the game her father taught her as a little girl that always kept her entertained. First, she would pick someone out of a crowd to observe, and then she would create a life for them: who they were, where they were going and coming from, what kinds of jobs they had, whether they were married or divorced, and so on. She stopped at a bench and smiled to herself, thinking of Harry's contribution to the game: undergarments. God, she missed Harry. He was the best of her.

Adelyne looked over at the lounge, packed with Christmas travelers. Dare she go in and order a glass of wine? A woman in her late sixties who only drank wine with dinner. Restaurants, bars, and cocktail lounges always provided a fun cast of characters. Sitting on the bench, she pushed her beautiful gray hair back from her face, which she always did when feeling nervous or challenged.

A man standing inside the lounge, directly in front of the out-of-place Christmas tree, caught her eye. Good candidate, Adelyne thought, tossing the last drop of coffee along with the cup into the garbage can. She checked her watch again. Plenty of time before her granddaughter's plane arrived.

Gracefully she glided into the lounge looking for her subject. "Darn," she said out loud. The man had gone. Before she had the chance to find a new subject, the lights decorating the beautiful Christmas tree caught her eyes. Each light held an artificial candle inside water, which created small bubbles that swam to the top as the lights blinked on and off. She smiled, feeling an inner glow as bright as the lights on the tree. Instantly, she remembered the first time she'd had the pleasure of seeing lights just like these: Philips Department Store. They could not possibly be the same kind, Adelyne thought, moving closer to the tree for a better look.

Philips Department Store, had been the attraction on Main Street some forty years ago in the small town of Bridgeport, where she was raised. Adelyne reached her long, slender fingers toward one of the lights and received an intense jolt when she touched it. Had she been electrocuted? Her body was thrown backward into a long, black hole at lightning speed, and she found herself standing in the middle of an aisle at Philips Department Store. Suddenly she was standing mesmerized in front of the Christmas tree at Philips, with the newest sensation, "Christmas Bubble Lights." A group of children and adults stood around admiring the tree, especially the lights. Adelyne was a tall eleven-year-old who was bright for her age; most people thought so, as did Adelyne herself. She spotted her mother at the other end of the aisle, yelled, "Mom!" as she ran toward her. It wasn't a mature thing to do, but Philips was having a special on the lights, and she simply had to inform her mother immediately.

"Mother, you must see these new, most fantastic lights. We have to have them, we simply must!" Adelyne could tell by the look on her mother's face that she had done something her mother disapproved of, and she was right. Mother had a superior way of looking at you—and then, of course, there was her superior tone of voice.

"Adelyne, young ladies do not run through a department store yelling. Now calm yourself and speak." Again, she tried to explain how they had to buy these "Christmas Bubble Lights" and just how wonderful they were, but Mother was not having any of it. "Darling, the only thing I have to do is die and pay taxes," Mother said, as she continued her shopping, not the least bit interested in the lights.

"How original," Adelyne said under her breath, making sure Mother did not hear but satisfied with herself for saying what she felt. She reached into her skirt pocket, felt for the dime her father had given her yesterday, and headed to the soda fountain for a hot chocolate. Philips made the very best hot chocolate at the fountain, topped off with plenty of baby marshmallows and whipped cream.

As Adelyne waited for her hot chocolate, she tried hard not to be disappointed over the lights. *I must not think of this now*, she thought. I have so many things to work on at the moment. She dug into the whipped cream, thinking about the person or persons who were responsible for dropping off the baskets of baked goods every year at Christmas. For as long as she could remember, one of her neighbors would bake and then deliver approximately twenty baskets to surrounding neighbors. The mysterious baker was absolutely the best in the world. Inside the baskets were banana-walnut loaf, peach cobbler that melted in your mouth, and fudge brownies. She got weak just thinking about them. She took a long sip of her hot chocolate and promised herself that this year would be different. By hook or by crook, Adelyne Dancer was going to solve the mystery that had confounded Bridgeport for years: to reveal the identity of the Baking Santa Claus.

Pretending not to hear the soft whistle her mother used when trying to track her down, Adelyne decided she was not going to run at her mom's beck and call. How ladylike was that? After all, what was she, a dog? No, she would take a minute and continue to work on her plan. There was a mystery to be solved and, apparently, she was the only one in this town capable of handling the challenge.

On the way home from Philips, Adelyne could not hide her disappointment in her mother for not buying the most exciting thing to happen to a Christmas tree since popcorn—Christmas Bubble Lights. But she stayed focused, like a good sleuth should and decided to question her mother for clues in uncovering the Basket Baking Santa.

"Mother, do you remember the first time the Christmas baskets were delivered?"

"Oh, before you were born, about fourteen years ago," her mother replied, keeping her eyes on the road.

"Aren't you the least bit curious about who is making them?" Adelyne asked, watching her mother's face and thinking how beautiful she was. She shared no strong, physical characteristics with her mother, and, though she was crazy about her father, she wished she looked more like her mother. Dad was "a tall glass of water," with a long, thin face, brown eyes, and brown hair—not exactly handsome, but certainly not unattractive. Mother, on the other hand, was a beauty, and, as Adelyne got older, she realized she would have preferred to be more like her.

"How long has Mrs. Ryan been a widow?" Adelyne asked. Her mother always took a moment before answering a question. This could be annoying at times to an eleven-year-old girl, but Mother always insisted on thinking before you spoke.

Her mother finally answered the question as they pulled into their driveway. "Fifteen. Buddy Ryan died fifteen years ago."

Adelyne jumped out of the car and ran to pick up the large acorns that had fallen onto their lawn. "I need at least four more," she thought, as she scooped them up and then skipped up the walkway.

"Snow, I want it to snow," Adelyne sang as she danced in front of the house, dropping an acorn as she did. Running back over to help her mother with the packages, Adelyne asked another question. "What does Mr. Martin do?"

Her mother handed her two packages before answering. "I think he's retired, dear." Adelyne left the house with a quick good-bye. She had a list of three names. All of them were possible suspects, and Adelyne was on a mission. She decided the Christmas Baker had to be either Mrs. Ryan, Mr. Martin, or Ruby Marco. All three of them had lived in the town for a very long time, all were at home most of the day, and all were very sweet people.

Mrs. Ryan's son had gone off to college many years ago and returned to town only for an occasional visit. The cottage where she lived had been her home—the place where her husband, Buddy, had been born and died. It was a lovely house, and Adelyne always liked to stop off to visit. As she walked down the Ryans' sloping walkway, she could easily imagine the garden that bloomed magnificently every spring: roses of various colors, lilies—pure white—and sunflowers as tall as Adelyne. Oh, Mrs. Ryan had the most beautiful garden in town.

Adelyne reminded herself that she was there on business and should not be thrown off by Mrs. Ryan's charms, as she watched her delicate hands pour tea into a beautiful Christmas cup. Occasionally, Mrs. Ryan would push the hair from her face while answering questions without blinking an eye. "No darling, my son lives in Boston, not Atlanta."

"Then it's your sister who lives in Atlanta?" Adelyne sipped her tea in the most grown-up fashion.

"Maybe you're thinking of Ruby Marcos. She has a sister in Georgia, but I was an only child," Mrs. Ryan said, as she started folding laundry that was sitting on the couch, completely aware of Adelyne's intentions. Smells of apples and cinnamon filled her house, and the signs and sounds of Christmas burst from the small cottage.

Adelyne's senses were alive with the warmth of the season. She marveled at the red curtains, green lace tablecloths, gold Christmas napkins, and many years of knickknack collection, all of which created a wonderland of Christmas dreams. She should have asked many more questions about the suspects, but she had been much more interested in the decorations and the feeling of love inside the house. She made a mental note to put Mrs. Ryan at the top of the Santa Baker list.

Satisfied with the information she was able to obtain from Mrs. Ryan's, she hurried toward the railroad tracks, hoping to find Mr. Martin walking his dog, Pete. And here they were, coming to greet her. Pete was never on a leash, and he raced toward Adelyne with the exuberance of a dog who loved affection. Mr. Martin was a very funny man in his late sixties who still had a bounce in his step.

"How old is Pete?" Adelyne asked, in an attempt to lead into her real questions.

"Old Pete is ten, which is seventy in dog years."

"Oh," she said matter-of-factly. "Isn't that when you came to town?"

"No, I came to town fourteen years ago." Adelyne immediately added Mr. Martin at the top of the list. What a coincidence that he came to town the same year the baskets started appearing on all her neighbors' doorsteps. She walked with Mr. Martin past the river as he told her about his four children. One of them lived in South Carolina, which was close enough to the peach state for him to send Mr. Martin peaches or peach filling to make cobbler.

"Are you hoping for a white Christmas?" Mr. Martin asked.

"Oh, most definitely!" she said, looking up to the sky and crossing her fingers as she made a wish for snow. She waved good-bye to Mr. Martin and realized that she was not any closer to uncovering the Santa Claus Baker. She woke up to the smell of coffee and the sound of her mother's voice telling her father to have a good day. Tomorrow was Christmas Eve, and Adelyne was excited with all of the possibilities that vacation and the season brought to her life.

Last night, her father had cleared an area in the living room where they would put up the tree they were going to buy tonight. She walked to the vacant area and spun around once. Two full days and so much to do. *I am beginning to sound like my mother, and I have not even reached my teens*, she thought.

Her mother had a bowl of oatmeal and a cup of warm apple cider waiting for her at the kitchen table. "Mother, you made it absolutely clear that *Ruby* had to trim my hair, didn't you?" Silence. "Mother?"

"I simply refuse to answer that question again," her mother said, without much emotion.

"Well, I'll die if they give me anyone other than Ruby."

"We'll miss you," Mom said, as she poured herself a cup of coffee.

Ruby was a woman with the most beautiful hair, and according to some people, the biggest heart in town. She worked as a part-time hairdresser at Bee's Beauty Parlor on Maple and Main. An attractive woman—albeit in an obvious way—she had ruby-red hair, lots of makeup, and a full figure.

The minute that Adelyne sat in the chair for her trim, she brought up the subject of baking. Ruby ran over to the tray of Christmas cookies that she baked for the customers. *This was going to be easy*, Adelyne thought: *The Santa Baker was Ruby with the big heart.*

She looked at the cookies. They looked a lot like the ones her mother made, and Adelyne was not very impressed. Picking out a cookie was the easy part, but finishing these not-very-tasty piles of dough was another thing altogether. As Ruby talked nonstop about everything under the sun, Adelyne rethought her list of possible suspects and felt like a total failure. Mrs. Ryan had a lovely house that smelled wonderful, but she hadn't been baking or cooking anything. In fact, Mrs. Ryan had told her that she had no goodies to offer her. Mr. Martin revealed many things about himself, including that he had a hard time making hard-boiled eggs, which was why he ate most of his meals at the diner. Ruby—well, Ruby knew everything about everything, except how to make a good cookie.

Her mother came into the beauty parlor, and it struck Adelyne that she was the most beautiful woman in the room. Smiling, Mom told Adelyne how pretty and mature the hairstyle made her look. Mother had a way of making everything okay, and when they got home, they sat at the dining room table to put the finishing touches on the acorns they'd just painted. The two of them spent the rest of the afternoon pulling out the Christmas ornaments from the basement and dusting them off. These were the best times with Mother, whom she knew loved her without question. Mom was smart, funny, and beautiful, yet she could always make you feel like you were all those things, too. Dad was lucky to have married her, and Adelyne was lucky to have her as a mother.

It was Christmas Eve, and the tree was in the living room, standing in front of the bay window, where they would be decorating it tonight. She could hardly contain her excitement as she helped her mother around the house.

Adelyne had a new plan to bring to light who the Santa Claus Baker was. She rubbed her hands together and congratulated herself. Stepping outside the front door onto the porch, she carefully hung bells at the top of the stairs, four in a row, like holly. Whoever came up the stairs to the porch would run into the bells on the way up. And that way, Adelyne would unravel the fourteen-year-old mystery.

Mother prepared pork chops with apples, walnuts, and a stuffing that Dad could never get enough of. They all sat and talked about driving to Gram's in the morning, when her mother and dad pretended that they had forgotten to buy presents. Adelyne found this funny because, for the first time in three years, she had not searched the house for gifts. She had devoted so much effort to finding out about the Christmas baskets, she had completely forgotten, which was not like her.

Changing the subject, she asked her parents whether they thought it was stupid for someone to go to the trouble of making baskets and then not allow anyone in town to know who he or she was.

"No," Dad answered. "That is the true spirit of Christmas. Remember, 'God so loved the world that he gave his only son.'" Adelyne helped her mother clean up the kitchen, inspired by the idea of giving without expecting much in return. By the time they joined her dad in the living room, the lights were on the tree. They were the Christmas Bubble Lights from Philips Department Store, and Adelyne was unable to take her eyes off of them for hours. Dad read "The Night before Christmas," and Adelyne eventually fell asleep on the couch, her eyes following each bubble to the top of its light.

On Christmas morning, Adelyne woke before anyone else. She walked over to the tree and turned on the lights. Then she opened the front door and found a beautiful basket of baked goods. Placing the basket under the tree, Adelyne admired the floating bubbles and said a prayer with each bubble that raced to the top. After a moment, she reached for the light, hoping to capture a dream.

The shock of the bright airport lights, as well as the cacophony of the many travelers, brought her back to the present. She felt a jolt of melancholy for her parents, who had been gone from this world for quite some time. She stepped back from the tree and smiled at the lights and the world that they had allowed her to visit. Checking her watch, she realized her granddaughter's flight had landed several minutes earlier. Adelyne turned and made it to the gate just in time to watch her granddaughter walk out and step into the warmth of her grandmother's arms.

"Mommy said to save some peach cobbler for her and Dad," her granddaughter said, smiling.

"You bet I will." Walking hand in hand, Adelyne thought of Mrs. Ryan and how Adelyne eventually discovered that the kind woman was the Santa Claus Baker. Adelyne found out that it was Mrs Ryan the year Mrs Ryan got sick and asked Adelyne for help. Now Adelyne carried on the tradition, and she hoped her granddaughter would find it important enough to do the same, giving without the thought of receiving.

Observing the woman as she stepped away from the Christmas tree, Sandy Parker took a long drag on his cigarette. He took a sip of his beer and contemplated the glow that seemed to emanate from her body. Sandy had always experienced the holiday season with quiet reserve and envied people who were filled with joy. His turbulent childhood had left him without much religious education, and Christmas had never meant much to him. For Sandy, Santa Claus was just an old white man who never came through with his promises.

Trying to quit smoking had been rough, but Sandy was now down to three cigarettes a day. Thankfully, drinking had never been a big problem, even when he was running wild in the streets. Sandy was glad he was still able to drink a couple of beers socially and not feel any negative effects.

The lights on the tree were beautiful, and, though the tree seemed out of place in the lounge, Sandy had to admit that it was gorgeous. He smiled, quite satisfied with himself for finding enjoyment in the lavishly decorated Christmas tree. There had been a time in his life when nothing was enjoyable, nothing at all. Sandy got off the bar stool and walked over to the tree, which he felt was calling to him. "Wow! What a beautiful tree!" Sandy felt the words slide from his lips, surprised that the voice was his own. He admired the individual ornaments and was amazed at the variety of decorations. Topping the tree was a papier-mâché angel with a hand-painted face that looked as if it had been done by a child. The sight of the angel caught Sandy off guard, and he stood staring into the angel's face. What a time that was, he thought, moving around the tree. He glanced around to see whether anyone was watching him. Confident that no one was nearby, he reached up and took the angel off the top of the tree. He immediately felt his equilibrium slip away.

"Why am I so damn nervous?" Sandy kept repeating as he stood admiring the Christmas tree in the living room of the Livingstons' house. The angel at the top had captured his attention. The tree was filled with otherwise very expensive ornaments, among which the papier-mâché angel with the hand-painted face looked out of place.

It had been a pretty good year for Sandy financially. Twelve months ago, he had given up his street attitude and dead-end jobs to work security for his friend Benny, an ex-cop. Now, the money was coming in, and Sandy found he was good at his job. People liked him, Benny said, because he had eyes in the back of his head.

Bryan Livingston, a popular newscaster, had employed Benny to monitor several of his frequent parties, and Benny had hired Sandy to help out. Tonight was the Christmas party for Livingston's employees. Benny wanted him to bring a date to the party, since they were supposed to be employees, but Sandy did not know any woman he felt comfortable bringing to a place like this. Sandy had the habit of dating the worst kind of people. He felt he could not get hurt emotionally if he knew up front that they were players. So, although things were coming together financially, his personal life was still a mess. He was thirty years old and had never really known love of any kind. His mother had died when he was a toddler, and he had bounced from foster home to foster home. Christmas made him nervous. Sandy was afraid that someone at the party would ask him questions that would make him feel the way he had as a child: like an orphan. He told himself he needed to think positively, that this was going to be his year. Sandy liked his job, and he was taking a night class on "positive thinking and transforming your life." *Okay*, he thought, *start to circulate*. This is a party, and you're supposed to be a guest. He began moving through the crowd, sipping ginger ale from a champagne glass. As he watched the Livingstons greet guests, feeling the warmth from the fireplace as he walked past, Sandy wished he had a home with a wife and children. There was nothing worse than having his emotions locked inside, only to have them come out as anger. *Keep focused*, he thought, making his way to the food. It was a simple job, really: Just make sure that none of the guests walked off with any valuables. When Sandy told acquaintances what he did, they all reacted the same way. "Why invite people to your house, if you think they will steal from you?" After laughing, he would remind them how often they had taken things when there was not much to steal. Then he told them stories about how frequently thefts happened at these types of homes with so many caterers and the other help. Sandy moved to the food table and surveyed the spread: shrimp cocktail, caviar, crab cakes, and deviled eggs. "Great layout," he said to the server, trying hard to be a celebrant. But before he could start filling his plate, his heart skipped a beat and his palms got sweaty. It was Maryanne Alister, and she was a vision! Maryanne was a producer for several segments on the newscast. She had been at another party he worked, but they had not been introduced. She was wearing a white dress, and her skin looked like chocolate silk. Sandy was utterly done in by her smile and her smell. Here was a woman who was in a league of her own, and he knew he could not touch her.

Benny's voice broke into his thoughts. "Circulate." Partygoers were supposed to be downstairs only, so Sandy walked to the game room, where a large pool table, a virtual-reality game, and several pinball machines were set up. Nothing to steal there. Moving on, Sandy scanned the room quickly so he could get back to the living room—and to Maryanne Alister. When he got back to the living room, a pianist was playing Christmas carols and Maryanne was organizing several people to sing. She motioned for him to join. "I'm no singer," he said and backed up. What an idiot, he thought, feeling more and more like a schoolboy and less like security.

Time moved quickly, but Sandy wanted to pause every moment he was in Maryanne's presence. The pianist and the caroling were replaced by the sophisticated sound system throughout the house. Sandy walked back to the Christmas tree, frustrated with his inability to be charming and warm.

"That is a beautiful angel, don't you think?" Sandy faced the speaker and saw with pleasure that Maryanne had asked the question. Sandy stood for a moment without speaking and then blurted,

"Do you like the face?" His tone implied that he did not.

"Oh, yes," Maryanne replied. "Looks like a face that a child would paint. Innocent." They laughed and talked about nothing, but about everything. She was warm and real and had the special quality of making whomever she was talking to feel like the most important person in the room. "What do you think of when you think of Christmas?" Maryanne asked him.

"Family." After he said it he felt goofy, but her next question made him feel that she could read his heart.

"Past, present, or future?"

Before he had a chance to answer, someone was touching his arm. Bryan Livingston was bringing the party to a close by handing out small ornaments to each of his guests. Sandy looked down at an ornament of a praying Santa Claus. He looked up to show Maryanne, but she was gone. *Oh God*, he thought, *I'm just like the prince after Cinderella disappears*. He dreaded the thought of never seeing her again.

Benny gave him the evil eye, and Sandy did a once-around through the downstairs to make sure that no one was walking off with anything.

"Damn," Sandy said aloud, causing heads to turn in his direction. Maryanne was gone. How could it be that a woman he'd known for one night could give him this feeling in his heart, one that he had never known before? Embarrassed by having drawn attention to himself, Sandy found he was fighting back tears.

"Hey, there you are." Sandy turned at the sound of Maryanne's voice. His heart lit up like the Christmas tree nearby. "I wanted you to have this," she said, handing Sandy the wrapped ornament that Mr. Livingston had given her.

"Thank you." He was a little confused and wasn't sure whether he should offer her the ornament he got. Man, how he wanted to say something witty in order to get her phone number, but there were no words, and before he could react, she was gone again.

Benny and Sandy inspected the property to make sure that everyone had left. Walking around the house, he could not get his chin off the floor, thinking he would never see her again.

Mr. Livingston thanked them for a job well done. Sandy asked him whether he could take a closer look at the angel at the top of his tree, and Bryan obliged without much thought. Sandy needed a minute and struggled with the small ornament in the box that Maryanne had given him.

What appeared to be a white piece of paper floated to the floor. It landed face up, and Sandy saw that it was a business card from Maryanne Alister. Smiling, Sandy took the ornament out of the box. It was just like the angel on the top of the tree. He looked at the angel's face, which he now loved.

As he touched it with the tips of his fingers, he found himself back in the middle of the crowded airport lounge.

"Do you believe in angels?" asked the woman standing behind him. Sandy turned, and, with a grin as bright as the lights on the tree, responded, "Yes; yes, I do," to a very pregnant Maryanne Alister Parker. The couple clasped hands and walked out of the lounge, heading for home.

"I'll tell you, Mom—our little Daniel is at home counting the hours till Santa arrives." Maryanne laughed and pulled him closer.

Marc Andrea just couldn't figure out what was going on in front of that Christmas tree, but everyone who stopped and touched it seemed to become hypnotized by it. He felt foolish at the thought, but to him it was as if they had been transported. In fact, one lady had stood there for at least twenty minutes. Maybe it was all the business traveling he had been doing. Marc walked over to the tree and looked it over very carefully. After a moment, he grabbed his briefcase and left the lounge. Just a nice, well-decorated, out-of-place Christmas tree, he thought, heading for his gate.

The End

Don't forget to be kind to strangers; for some who have done this have entertained angels without knowing it!

HEBREWS 13:2

Gloria Diamond sat on the edge of her bed, looking at the digital time on the AM/FM radio alarm clock on her night table. At 7:07 p.m. on Christmas Eve, it was time to get ready for the night shift at 911. She reached for the pack of Marlboros next to the clock. As she got out of bed, she stubbed her toe on the dresser, which was too large for her bedroom.

"Damn," she said loudly, as she hit the switch that turned on the overhead light. Gloria had been renting the two-bedroom, one-bath California bungalow for over two years, and there were many things she planned to update, once she got the time. But, as with a good many of her intentions, time had run out on fixing the place. The bank informed her a week ago that they had taken it back as an REO (Real Estate Owned), and she had thirty days to vacate. She hated the light in the bathroom; it was much too bright, but any wattage lower than one hundred made it tough for her to put on her makeup. So, every day she would walk into the bathroom and whisper the same words, "Got to do something about this light."

Holding her dyed-blond hair back from her face, Gloria wondered what happened to the homecoming queen as she examined the lines and dark circles around her eyes. Too many bad choices, she guessed, lighting a cigarette and taking a long drag. She performed the same routine every day, and she laughed, knowing it was her mother's bathroom habits she copied. "Always look the face over and then promise yourself a better diet, less partying, and more exercise."

Gloria had to smile, thinking of her mother and grandmother. They were a tag team, and when all three of them were together, Gloria never felt like there was enough room for her. Mom and Grandma caused such a scandal when Gloria was attending Catholic school in the valley during the sixties. She took another drag on the cigarette, laughing out loud at the thought of her mother coming into church in white go-go boots and a miniskirt. Right alongside her mother was Grandma, in her fake leopard coat and washed-out blond cotton-candy hair. Most of the girls at school thought the two of them were the rage, but Gloria was always a bit embarrassed. Well, that was where she gotten her vanity, Mom and Grandma. As it turned out, all three of them had been married and divorced twice. Not a good thing. Nope; not a good thing at all.

Gloria poured herself a cup of coffee and watched the blinking, colored lights on the small artificial tree that was standing on top of the television. When Gloria was a little girl, she always promised herself she would never become like Nanny and Gramps Kelly, who always had small trees sitting on top of their television. She would stay overnight, and they would never put the lights on because it would interfere with Grandpa watching TV. Now, here she was with the same setup. Gloria left the light on in the living room as she walked out the front door, running ten minutes late as usual. She got into her tank of a car parked on the street in front of the house, hoping it would start. After a quick prayer, she turned her key, and the engine turned over on the first try. Gloria knew she talked to God only when she needed or wanted something for herself, and she felt a sudden tinge of shame. The small houses on her tiny cul-de-sac had all been decorated with some form of exterior lights, except, of course, her house, but she critiqued the houses harshly as she drove down the street, wondering why most had bothered to decorate at all.

It was business as usual when she arrived at her faceless cubicle, which was void of any single personality due to twenty-four hour shifts and multiple occupants. She dropped her purse and got herself a cup of coffee. It was one stressful job, but pretending that it was all just a reality-based television show helped her cope. Heck, nobody had better denial skills than Gloria.

That was how she was able to let her first husband take her son and move to Texas, without the tiniest fight from her. Her excuse was that he was better off—which was probably the truth. Still, it had helped her sleep easier during the past ten years. Denial was why she thought she'd lasted so long at 911.

The first couple of calls were standard, but then the night began to come alive. "Nine one one. What is the nature of your emergency?" she said.

"I'm looking for my brother," came the slurred voice of a man who had to be under the influence of alcohol or drugs.

"This is nine one one, sir."

"I just got out, and I need to talk to my brother. Can you help me find him?"

"I am sorry, sir, but this is nine one one. Have you tried directory assistance?"

"Of course I did." This time his voice was raised, and he was quickly becoming incensed. "But the government has hidden him from me! You have to help me! I know nine one one is government controlled, you lousy…" *Jeez, this world was getting worse every day*, Gloria thought, as she took a quick sip of coffee and answered the next call. A woman was sobbing on the line, and Gloria tried to calm her down in order to help her. "Miss, please, can you take a breath?" After several minutes, she was able to get the caller to calm down enough to tell her what happened.

"My boyfriend beat me up and threw me out of the apartment. I think he broke my nose." Gloria began to extract standard information from her as the woman interjected several details. "I'm at the phone by the 7-Eleven on Oxnard. It's next door to where I live."

"Are you safe at the moment?" Gloria asked.

"All of this happened because I burned the chicken." Again, the woman started to cry hysterically, and then, suddenly, she started to scream. It sounded like someone was beating her up.

The night had gotten off to a horrible start, and Gloria could not detach herself from the people who needed her help. She was able to send a squad car out to the woman whose boyfriend had beaten her, but not before he had hurt her severely. The next call was from a hysterical child whose father had shorted out a light socket and set their Christmas tree on fire while hanging lights at the last minute.

Gloria sat in the break room wanting a cigarette and drinking coffee, not feeling her usual self. If she had been disappointed with past Christmases, they were nothing compared to how she felt tonight. Everything was affecting her in a very personal way. She rested her head on the back of the chair, with her feet stretched out in front of her. A coworker walked into the break room and said, "Merry Christmas," as she put coins in the vending machine that offered soda pop in cans. Not wanting to talk, Gloria kept her eyes closed and tried to remember when she began avoiding Christmas in any meaningful or spiritual way.

Thoughts of the fourth grade and the Christmas mailbox she was in charge of making for her class, as well as the Christmas card exchange, made her smile. She never thought she would miss Catholic school when she was a student, but now she felt nostalgic for the celebrations, especially Christmas. Remembering that particular Christmas helped ease the anxiety that had accompanied her to the break room just a few minutes earlier.

Sister Elizabeth had given her the task of making the Christmas mailbox, and Gloria made three different versions before she was able to settle on the one she took to school. It was the first Christmas that Gloria had not believed in Santa Claus. With Santa out of the picture, she found herself paying more attention to the birth of Christ and the origin of the season. Strange. In retrospect, she could see that time as a very important transition in her young life. Back then, everything about God made sense to her. Gloria began listening to hymns rather than carols.

As she opened her eyes in the antiseptic break room, the bright light made her squint. She checked her watch; it was time to get back to the switchboard.

The cubicle was as Gloria had left it. Staring at the red lights that needed answering, she put the headset back on. "Please, Lord, help me with these calls," Gloria prayed silently, as she answered the first call.

"Nine one one. What is the nature of your emergency?" A weeping man was on the other end of the telephone, and Gloria tried to get him to speak to her. After several minutes, the man revealed to her that he had a gun pointed at his head and just needed to say something to someone before he pulled the trigger.

Gloria's heart seemed to leap out her chest, but she got the man to speak. Nothing mattered to her more than the red light on the board. If she could just think of the red light and not the man, she would be able to address the problem in a professional manner. But she could not because he was not a red light; he was a man, a desperate man. She immediately dispatched the police to go to his address.

She felt she was babbling. She heard herself say something about everyone being connected to each other. I must have lost my mind, Gloria thought to herself, as she continued talking about how important it was to her for him not to end his life tonight. The sound of his cynical laugh brought her out of the trance like state, as she tried desperately to convince him to put the gun down and open the door for the police.

Looking up, she realized her supervisor was standing behind her with another coworker, and Gloria thought she was finished for the way she was handling the call.

"Okay," came the voice from the other end of the telephone line. After several seconds, Gloria realized the man had put the gun down and opened the door for the police. One of the officers informed her that everything was okay. She pulled the headset down around her neck and looked apprehensively at her boss.

"He's okay," she uttered, afraid he was going to fire her on the spot.

"Good job! Take a breather and then come on back," was all he said. She sighed with relief.

The night moved quickly, and the intensity of the trouble subsided. Gloria thought of Christmas. She missed so many things about the holiday that she had not allowed herself to think about in quite some time: Midnight mass with Mom and Grandma, the school plays with everyone wanting to play Mary and Joseph but always having to be shepherds or people at the inn, and all the people who had been in her life who were now gone from her thoughts, until tonight.

The red light flashed, and Gloria answered. "Nine one one. What is the nature of your emergency?"

"I think something happened to Santa Claus," said the squeaky voice on the other end of the line. Her initial instinct was to think it was a prank, but something in the voice made her pursue the call further.

"What?" she inquired.

"I think something *bad* happened to Santa!" Gloria realized that the child was upset and that it was not a prank telephone call from some kids messing around."Why do you say that?" The child was crying, but then seemed to regroup and try to speak more clearly. Gloria realized it was a young girl—she guessed around seven? Eight?

"I—I was driving with my friend's mother tonight, and we saw some guys beating up on Santa, but my friend's mother said it was just a store Santa, not the real one. But I don't think so." More tears.

After waiting several seconds, Gloria asked the only thing she could think of. "How do you know it was not just a store Santa—which is just as bad," she added quickly."Because he never came to our apartment, and my little sister and brother are going to be sad." Looking down at her watch, Gloria realized it was five o'clock in the morning and that Santa probably was not coming to the little girl's house.

"Is your mom at home?"

"She's sleeping," the young girl said, through sniffles.

Gloria sat for a moment, speechless, and then asked, "What did your mom say about Santa?" She heard her wiping her nose before answering.

"Not to count on him—he's just like our father." That was it. Tears began running down Gloria's face as she copied down the little girl's address from the computer screen.

"Do me a favor. Go back to sleep and keep your brother and sister asleep with you, because I just saw Santa fly over my building, and you know he cannot stop while children are awake. Will you do that for me?" Silence. "Will you do that for me, honey?"

"Okay," came the reply, and then the sound of a telephone being put back on the receiver.

The next shift began arriving, and Gloria relinquished her post. She uttered quick good-byes to those within earshot and ran out to her car. It did not start immediately this time. She lit a cigarette and began to cry as she thought of the children and the hard realities of life they unfortunately had to experience. After several prayers and a few more turns of the ignition, the car started. Gloria sat there for a moment and looked at the address she had written down earlier.

Pulling out of the parking lot, Gloria glanced at her watch. It was 5:35 a.m.—not much time. She drove toward the Save-On store she passed five days a week. She thought of all the choices she had made because they were the easy ones, like not seeing her son enough or avoiding her relationship with God.

Gloria decided not to make an easy choice tonight. Save-On was one of those giant pharmacies that, in all actuality, served as an all-purpose convenience store. As she got out of the car, Gloria felt relieved at the sign that said in big bold letters: "Open twenty-four hours."

Inside, a security guard was talking to the night manager, who looked like he wanted nothing more than to sleep. Within minutes, Gloria had filled a wagon with toys and games and solicited help from the two men. While one of the men wrapped the gifts, the other wrote out cards from Santa Claus, as she told them the story of the children. She paid for the gifts with the remaining $200 she had on her credit card and asked the guard to help her out to the car. Again, the car took several attempts to start, but it finally did, and she was on the road, wondering whether she could really be fired for taking the address off the computer. It mattered, but she was not going to turn back.

The neighborhood was run-down, and the apartment building was in worse condition than she had imagined. Pulling into the driveway, she left her car running, with the headlights on, as she looked for the manager's apartment.

"What are you doing?" Gloria kept repeating to herself as she stood telling the startled, aging manager the story.

"Leave the gifts at the door," said the man, agitated about being disturbed. "Please, sir, it's Christmas. We'll just drop the gift right inside the door. Come on! Children have to believe in something. If they can't believe in the spirit of Christmas…" Gloria had not meant to break down, but tears began to roll down her face, and there was no stopping them as she struggled to say, "Then, what chance do they have?"

He looked at her like she was crazy and asked whether she had been drinking, but he eventually opened the door. "Mother's a drug addict; older girl always taking care of the younger two," he said quietly. The apartment was dark, and Gloria dropped the presents inside the front door and left, as she said she would.

Driving home, she remembered the Christmas cards she had written out and the meaning of the season that they tried to capture: "Glory to God in the highest and peace to his people on earth." Gloria spent the day in bed the way she normally did on a work day. The alarm went off and the routine started, as it did on most days, except now, Gloria started with a prayer that she could help one person on the switchboard tonight.

The cubicle was empty when she arrived. Gloria set the Christmas card down on the desk in front of her. It read, "Glory to God in the highest and peace to his people on earth!" She barely had time to get comfortable before the lights began to flash. Running her hands over the outside of the card, she answered, "Nine one one. What is the nature of your emergency?"

The End

An Unexpected Gift

And a child will lead them all.

ISAIAH 11:6

Jesse Torres waited in the courtroom for the judge to call his name. He glanced over at his mother and knew she was still angry with him by the way she stared straight ahead at the judge. Mom had this nervous body language any time a family member was in crisis. She walked with stiff, robotic movements, and her eyes seemed to enlarge, like they were about to jump out of her head. During the past several weeks, before Jesse's court date, he pretended to all of "the boys" that he was not the least bit afraid. But, truth be told, he was scared. And sitting there next to his very nervous mother was making him even more nervous.

His mother and father were good parents—better than most. Yet at seventeen, Jesse could not get along with his father, or with any other male authority figure who tried to control him. How many arguments in the last month did he have with Poppy? (This was the nickname his mother said Jesse gave his father when he was two years old.) All Jesse wanted to do was to hang out with his friends, party a little, and date girls. He tried to tell his father that he wasn't a gangbanger or anything like that, but all Poppy ever did was to throw Jesse's friends and his trouble in his face.

"You think being in a gang will make you a man? You think carrying a gun makes you tough? Go to work every day, go to college, and then I'll respect you," his dad would say. Jesse had been arrested twice in the last four months, once for destroying school property and once for drinking and disturbing the peace, when he broke some windows in a vacant house. Here it was, the first week of December, and he had already been suspended from school five times.

"Jesse Torres!" The sound of his name echoed through the courtroom. It made him feel like a little boy, and he wanted to crawl into his mother's arms. She took his hand, but he quickly shook it loose. There was no time for that, not here. He might know someone. The judge's bench looked big and intimidating from where Jesse stood. His case was assigned to Judge Warner, the same white man he'd had from the beginning. Jesse did not like him, but his mother said he was a fair man, and that was all you needed. Warner addressed Jesse directly, locking eyes as he spoke and making Jesse feel like a trapped animal.

"Young man, this is the second and last time I'm going to see you. Do you understand me?" Jesse stood speechless. Warner was about to send him to juvenile hall, and now he was sorry that he had not stopped screwing around. "You have a good mother, son," Warner continued, "and that makes you very fortunate, because I know she is fighting for your well-being. I am going to give you a community service assignment instead of sending you to juvenile hall." Judge Warner picked up a piece of paper and looked down at it to examine the information. "It says here that you've been suspended from school for ten days." Jesse and his mother nodded. "Then you have a two-week Christmas holiday. Is that correct?"

"Yes," his mother answered quickly, and, happily, her tight movements and stiff head seemed to have relaxed. The tension had shifted from Jesse and his mother to the people behind them in the courthouse who were waiting their turn for judgment. "I'm telling you this as sincerely as I possibly can, young man. Do not make the mistake of appearing before me again, or I will hit you hard. I hope you learn something by giving back to the community during the next two months." Warner and Jesse's mother nodded to each other with mutual respect and agreement.

They were led over to the bailiff for Jesse's work-detail assignment. Jesse let his mother take the envelope from the clerk. He wondered what would happen if he did not show up for his work assignment. Before he had a chance to finish the thought, Judge Warner spoke to him. "Mr. Torres, if you miss one day, I will find you in contempt of this court and send you to juvenile hall. Believe me when I tell you—you will not like it there." Jesse looked at the judge, startled by Judge Warner, who seemed to have intercepted his thoughts and then threw them back at him to rethink.

When he stepped into the bright sunlight outside the courthouse, Jesse could hardly believe it was December. The street was crowded with people in a hurry. He and his mother made it over to a hotdog cart, getting a couple of dogs and a Coke for lunch.

"Did you see where I have to go?" Jesse asked, nervous with the prospect of this new challenge. His mother handed him her Coke and dug into her oversized purse for the envelope. They found seats on the wall outside the courthouse and enjoyed the seventy-degree Southern California weather.

The two of them opened the envelope. It read "Pony Express."

"It's a program for disabled children," his mother said, in between sips of her soda.

"I know, Mom. I can read," Jesse said, annoyed.

On the way home, his mother stopped at St. Mark's to light a candle. Jesse sat in the car just to spite her. His mother had asked him earlier to go with her to Saint Mark's to thank the Lord for being with them today. Of course, that started an argument. On the drive from the courthouse, his mother counseled him about his spiritual life, and how, if Jesse let him, Jesus could help. "If he really wanted to help me, why didn't he get me off scot-free?" Jesse said sarcastically.

His mother parked in the lot behind the beautiful, old church. She did not get upset with him the way his father did. When she got out of the car, all Mom did was say a brief word. "If you change your mind..." Jesse decided to sit out in the car and feel sorry for himself rather than give in to his mother's wishes. While driving home from church, his mother drove them past Little Mario's quadruplex, where Jesse's crew was hanging out in the small front yard of the property. Music was blaring through open windows, and he could see beer cans on the porch. None of them was a gang member, but Jesse knew some of them had the potential for big-time trouble. He slid down in the car to avoid being seen by any of them.

Jesse spent a fitful night and finally crawled out of bed near dawn, when he heard his father in the kitchen. Poppy was ready for work and making oatmeal when Jesse walked in. His father ate oatmeal every morning during the workweek, and Jesse joined him at the table for a bowl.

He was nervous about his first day at Pony Express. He watched the clock, the way he used to do as a young child. Jesse recalled hating his first year of school; he hadn't wanted to leave his mother.

The sound of the loud muffler outside their rented house announced that his father's ride to work had arrived. His dad's attention moved to the front door, and his parting words were, "Keep your mind open today. Good luck."

While watching his father walk out the door, Jesse thought how hard it was to grow up and let go of the needs that were typically thought of as childish. Everything inside of him wanted to jump up and run to the door, yelling, "I Love You, Poppy." But, of course, his pride and self-image of himself would not allow that to happen.

"Why are we leaving so early?" Jesse asked his mother, as she started the car, giving the 1974 Monte Carlo time to warm up.

"I'm not sure where we are going—it's better to be early than to be late." They sat for a moment in silence. "You don't want to make a bad impression," she added.

Jesse turned on his hard-guy attitude, and then slouched down in his seat. "I don't care what impression I make."

His mother backed out of the driveway. "Well, I do."

He hated being so close to becoming a man and yet needing his mother and father so much. Jesse felt like he could have been five years old and heading off to kindergarten. His heart sank when his mother pulled off Sunland Avenue and onto the dirt road, with a large sign for Pony Express. Why did he feel inadequate now, when he could walk the streets unafraid?

"It will be all right, Jesse," his mother said, as she pulled into one of the many parking spots. "Do you want me to come in with you?" Jesse looked at her like she had gone mad. Of course he wanted her to come in with him, but he would never admit it, or allow it.

Jesse completed paperwork in a small mobile home that served as the organization's office. He was given a brief synopsis of what would be expected of him. Karla, the woman in charge, was younger and prettier than Jesse expected.

"Your task is really very simple," she said. "You spot for the physical therapist who works with the child on either side of the horse. You also might be expected to carry one of the children to the horse, and, afterward, back to his parent."

Jesse walked down the sloping hill with several instructors who were leading their horses to the riding area. A few volunteers were already waiting when the group arrived at the riding site. Jesse wondered whether any of them were from the work program. The first of the children began to arrive, and Jesse watched the interaction between the volunteers and the children. It was obvious they knew each other well. Immediately, he felt like an outsider and wanted to slip away, but instead he sat on the bench far enough away to discourage conversation.

The morning was chilly, and Jesse wished he had brought a sweater or jacket. A young girl, about his age, came into the riding area and sat at the opposite end. Watching her discreetly, he was keenly aware that she was a new volunteer. He could tell by the stiffness of her body and the way she said "hello" to the parents. It was the way people greeted one another in a doctor's office or a courthouse. He leaned back and let his back press against the bench. He closed his eyes, and he wished he were anywhere but there. He began his favorite daydream, which was climbing a mountain.

"Jesse." The sound of his name made him jump, and he looked around for the person who had called him. A girl, about nineteen, who was apparently in charge of scheduling, was staring at him. He could not remember her name. "Spot for Jennifer," she said, looking from him to the area where Jennifer was working. Jesse looked at the other volunteer and then back to the girl with the clipboard.

"Why me?" he asked, a little embarrassed after the words came out of his mouth.

"I need someone strong to help with Brady," she stated, not looking up from her clipboard.

While walking out to the horse, he had to admit that he liked her answer. *Most people are trying to get over on you*, he thought silently to himself. Just as quickly, he heard his father's voice saying, "Jesse, why do you think like that?" *Damn*, he thought, *I can't get away from Poppy*.

Trying hard to get his walk down, in case anyone was watching, Jesse bopped over to the horse, in his best street strut. He felt uncomfortable and a little apprehensive when he reached Moonglow. He stroked her sides, not wanting to show he was afraid of her, but the truth was that he had never spent any time around horses, and he was uneasy. Damn, if he was honest with himself, he was downright afraid of them.

A child was sitting on the horse directly in front of the physical therapist, Jennifer. Brady was a puny little boy with severe cerebral palsy. Jesse had heard of cerebral palsy, but he had never been this close to anyone with the condition. He stepped back, slightly put off by the child's contortions, but he quickly regrouped when he realized that the little boy was staring down at him from the horse. Brady had a tiny face, with large green eyes that seemed lit from inside.

Jesse looked into his little face and smiled, and Brady smiled back at him. Jesse quickly picked up the rhythm of the activity. Jennifer stretched Brady's body with a variety of positions on the horse while encouraging him verbally. Jesse listened and watched. The half hour ended quickly, and Jennifer asked Jesse to carry Brady back to the woman he presumed was his mother.

The child felt to Jesse like a fragile piece of glass in his arms. The boy looked up into Jesse's face with total confidence. Feeling Brady's calves, Jessie realized his legs were different in size. His right leg was small, but kind of normal size, but the left leg was like a twig. The bones were unusually thin and brittle. Taking inventory of the tiny body he held in his arms, Jesse noticed that Brady's arms and hands curved inward toward the body in a clenched position.

Confusion and sorrow as well as total happiness filled his first week of work. His mother and father had always instilled in him that he should pray for people who were less fortunate than he was. Although Jesse had never heeded those words before, he now found himself praying for every child that he spotted for. The ironic thing about praying for the children was that at first, Jesse did it out of his own fear. Walking next to the horses, he found himself saying, "Oh Lord, please help me calm down. I am so nervous that I am having a hard time talking to the kids." It must have been a natural progression because he soon found himself praying for each child he met, and eventually he found himself having a lot of fun. One morning,

Jesse was working with a little boy named Chris, who had to use crutches to walk. The lesson started out typically, until the horse developed a really bad case of flatulence. Jesse began to blame Chris for the "passing of the gas," which Chris thought was hilarious, after he got over the initial shock of being accused of such "loud ones."

Before long, Jesse felt at home with the people from Pony Express, especially the children. Coming to work was becoming a positive in his life, and he began looking forward to each new day. Jesse no longer felt uncomfortable carrying the children to the horse and back to their parents. In fact, he used that time to say a quick prayer over them, and to tell them how cool he thought they were. Looking at these children and their disabilities, Jesse came to realize that their strength of spirit was bigger than their ailments.

Slowly, Jesse began to spend less and less time with "the boys" and more time at home with his family. One evening, he was sitting on the sofa and watching his family in action. His mother, who took great pride in the house, was hanging Christmas decorations with his two little sisters. Poppy was out in the garage getting the Christmas lights out of boxes to hang around the outside of the house, and Jesse went outside to see him.

"Hey, Jesse; I didn't realize you were home."

Smiling at his father, Jesse said, "You're getting an early start this year." His dad took the lights out of the original boxes. "Poppy, you're so organized. You have everything labeled."

Laughing, his father said, "Easier that way, Jesse." They stood in the garage getting out the lights and making small talk. Jesse wondered when it had all gotten so complicated. How do you move so far away from your parents emotionally that everything you say, or they say, is cause for a fight?

He looked at his father, wondering what he thought about inside when he was alone. His father was a strong man physically, from years of hard labor, but it had never made him bitter, and Jesse liked that about him.

They hung the lights on the outside of the house, even though it had gotten dark. Poppy had turned on all the floodlights to make it easier for them to see. Now, everyone was standing on the small front lawn, waiting for his father to turn on the switch, which he did, amid much applause. At the dinner table, his parents went silent when Jesse joined the family in prayer. His involvement in the dinner conversation was in direct contrast to his usual sulking; it centered on the children he had been working with every day.

Jesse was disappointed when Brady didn't show for his lesson. The boy came for therapy two times a week, and Jesse had really taken to him. Jesse's original thought was that Brady might have gone on Christmas vacation with his family, but Jesse found out later in the day that he had ended up in the hospital due to seizure activity. Jesse surprised himself by the feelings he had for Brady. He found out which hospital Brady was in and made it a point to visit him.

While Jesse was waiting for the bus, he heard a whistle. He looked up and saw Little Mario. Mario made an illegal turn in the middle of the street and pulled up to the bus stop. Several guys from the neighborhood were in the car.

"Get in. It's party time," Tito said, opening the door. The minute Jesse was inside the car, he realized he had made a mistake. Tito had an open beer, and there was a six-pack on the floor in the backseat. After a couple of minutes in the car, Jesse realized they were not heading toward the neighborhood.

"Where are you going?" he asked hesitantly.

"Relax and have a beer," Tito said, in charge as always.

"The valley," Little Mario added. Jesse tried hard to fit in, but in his heart, he did not want to be with them, looking for trouble.

"What are you doing in the valley?" Jesse asked, knowing his family was missing him for dinner.

"I got to pick up a car," Tito said, in between sips of his beer.

"Whose?" Jesse asked innocently.

Tito turned to him with a nasty smirk. "What, have you been hanging out with those retarded kids too long?" Tito paused dramatically before continuing. "Anybody's car I want!"

Little Mario pulled into a 7-Eleven for cigarettes, and Jesse quickly jumped out of the car.

"Where are you going, chump?" Tito demanded.

"Anywhere you're not," Jesse said. "And, Tito, those kids got more strength and spirit in one finger than you'll ever have." Some cops drove slowly by in a squad car, and, for the first time in his life, Jesse was glad to see them. The thought of all the challenges that those children faced made him feel small. How could he and his friends think their lives were so hard? How could he change that attitude?

Jesse wandered down the street aimlessly for a block or two. He then decided to find out where Saint Joseph's Hospital was located so he could go and see Brady.

He watched the Christmas lights on the storefronts from inside the warm bus and was reminded of home. Realizing that you could make yourself comfortable in your own skin by trying to do the right thing brought a smile to Jesse's face. He arrived at the hospital fifteen minutes before visiting time was over. Jesse stopped at the nurse's desk and asked for Brady's room. The floor was decorated with Christmas cheer, but it all seemed dreary. Hesitating at the door to the room, Jesse peered in and could see Brady's little body asleep in the bed. He stepped in. No one was there but Brady. After a few minutes, Brady's dad, Tom, came walking into the room with a cup of coffee in his hand. He was surprised and happy to see Jesse standing in the room. Tom gave him a rundown on Brady's health problems and all that had happened.

When visiting time ended, Tom offered Jesse a ride home. At first, Jesse declined. He told Tom that he lived far from the valley, but Tom insisted on taking him home. And so they became friends. Jessie learned that Brady didn't have a mother, and that the woman who sometimes brought Brady to Pony Express was a babysitter. While swapping stories on the way home, Jesse realized that he could learn a lot about himself from other people. He realized that what people wanted in life was not all that different from his own desires: happiness, peace, family, and a good friend.

Change comes whether you want it or not. Jesse knew it had come for him the moment he laid eyes on the children at Pony Express. He knew it when he began feeling more and more disconnected from his friends. After three weeks of working, he began socializing with many of the young volunteers and people from Pony Express. They were not the kind of people he first imagined them to be; they were fun and had good attitudes. Jesse decided his number-one goal should be to get his life at school together to make sure he would get a diploma. While growing up, Jesse always thought that you had to make a big impact. But it was more than that—it was the little things you did every day that made an impact. Like the way his father took care of his family, working hard to be an example of a good man. And the way Jennifer gave up big money at a private practice to work in a program that reached more children. Judge Warner could very easily have sent him to juvenile hall, but he had offered something else instead. Jesse looked around and realized he could go on and on. Examples were all around him, including his mother, who took care of her own as well as her husband's aging parents. They were all part of the solution, and Jesse wanted to belong to that club. He knew those children with their broken bodies and powerful spirits had given him an early Christmas gift, and he was determined to share it with the world, one small piece at a time.

The End

Angels in the Midst

God speaks of his angels as messengers swift as the wind and as servants made of flaming fire.

HEBREWS 1:7

D o you believe in coincidence? Coincidence is God's way of talking to you, so you should not think of it as anything less, and I hope this story will tell you why. In everyday life, events happen around us; some are monumental, some appear minor in nature, but all are connections to our true soul. Did you ever meet a stranger on a train who knew too much about your life, or meet a person you seemed to know but couldn't place? There is spiritual life all around us, and the majority of the time we don't recognize it as anything more than happenstance. Look around you; there are angels in your midst. You can call them by whatever name you want: guardian angels, good spirits, souls, or saints. But they are here to help and this is the story of one such angel, who is in the midst of your everyday life.

Chaz is an angel who has been working on earth for the last three centuries, and he, like most angels, goes way beyond the call of duty. Insightful artists have always been able to capture angels on canvas and, to a certain extent, they depict them accurately. The one thing about angels that most people don't understand is that they are under constant attack from the forces of evil. It is very dangerous for them to exchange their wings, even for a short time, to become humanlike. During this period, they are vulnerable to attack in a variety of ways. That is why we discourage angels from changing identities and only approve it when necessary. Remember this the next time you are in a crisis: the danger you encounter because of some events beyond your control, like the voice in your head that you think is intuition, or the stranger who helps and you never see again. What you have witnessed is not coincidence but the hard work of angels.

I know all this because I assign angels their duties. That brings us back to Chaz. He is not the most beautiful angel. In fact, his wings have been clawed up a few times in his fight against evil, but Chaz is the best at what he does, and his love of the human race makes him a great warrior. He has been with people when they cross over to our side, and he fights tooth and nail to make that happen. There are evil equivalents to angels, who make life the way it appears on the evening news. Believe otherwise and you will be misled. They are out there, and life is a constant battle, which we call "spiritual warfare." Angels are always fighting for your well-being.

The subway train pulled into the station, as Chaz made his way onto the platform, looking for Jennifer Carols. He flapped his tired wings in a constant wave of motion, creating a breeze of love. Looking around the platform, he saw that most of these people were under siege and needed his help.

Chaz smiled at a little girl holding her mother's hand. She recognized him, although he was invisible to most adults. She would learn shame in the process of growing up and would eventually forget the world as she saw it now. "It's just your imagination," her mother said, as she pulled the child into the subway car.

"No, it's not!" Chaz whispered to her, and he could see her face light up through the window of the train. Spreading his wings, he moved over the platform, looking for Jennifer, until he spotted her, angry and distraught, in the crowd.

Chaz boarded the train and scanned the passengers, but he did not sense any evil presence. He sat directly behind Jennifer and knew instantly that she was carrying a gun in her purse. He began to be flooded with images of what she planned to do. The angel observed the mixture of people on the train. It was two weeks before Christmas, and many people had shopping bags from stores, as well as wrapped gifts in hand. This is the season that the world celebrated the birth of the Lord, Chaz thought, and it was the best, but most volatile, time to be on earth.

Jennifer moved to the middle of the car and pushed hard to get a seat. Chaz surveyed the area, saw what could happen next, and began flapping his wings. Six bullets and they would all be hits—a bloody mess. The train car became standing room only, and Chaz had to make a decision. His wings informed him that there was evil in the area, but the force was not powerful. He hoped he could whisper in Jennifer's ear long and strong enough to change her mind.

Images of the potential tragedy kept coming to him, and he was afraid that if he did not change into a mortal, he could not prevent her from opening fire on the crowd. An angel could fight the degas tooth and nail in the spiritual world, but it was next to impossible to use physical force on a human unless you became one. Degas were from the "evil one," and they were responsible for planting the seeds of evil in everyday life. Their image was in stark contrast to angels, and they came in many physical forms, but they were easy to spot in true appearance. Degas were hideous creatures, who always had a tail—some short, some long—long claws and animal feet. Saliva continuously flowed, and they had a nasty odor that they could not hide, except as humans.

In an instant, Chaz decided to transform himself into a human in case he needed to stop her physically. Chaz took on the look of a white collar man, not a suit, but an office worker. Standing next to where she was sitting, he huddled in with the crowd as the subway pulled out of the station.

Chaz looked at the man sitting next to Jennifer, and an alarm went off inside him. He searched the man's eyes intently for the specks that were the usual traces of a transformation; it was a dega in human form!

The lights in the subway car went off and on as the train raced through the underground tunnels. Chaz felt he had failed with Jennifer. She had been an abused child, who became an abuser. Drug problems and a vicious temper had diminished her life for the last ten years, and she had been in and out of jail. Already a thief, she was now capable of murder. The angel eyed the dega, wondering if it had spotted him. At that moment, the dega looked up at him and showed its teeth.

Jennifer reached inside her bag and began yelling obscenities as she pulled out the semiautomatic. Chaz grabbed hold of her hand, which sent the first bullet through the roof of the train car. Passengers began screaming and dropped to the floor in panic. As Chaz fought for control of the gun, the dega got to its feet and began to fight the angel. For one second, time stood still on the train, as Chaz and the dega, who he knew to be Farshail, fought for the souls of the passengers in the line of fire.

"Let go, and I will make you a king!" the dega yelled. Chaz responded with a head butt that sent Farshail flying onto his back. Before Chaz was able to wrestle the gun out of Jennifer's hand, she fired two more shots. One knocked out a window, and the other went through the wall of the train.

In a flash, the dega was back up and on top of Jennifer and Chaz. It knew that two souls, who, if killed today, would come with it. Chaz and the dega continued to fight ferociously, sliding in and out of human and supernatural form as the lights of the train flickered on and off. The dega bit Chaz's hand and he let go of Jennifer for a moment. Chaz spread his wings, flapping with the force of hurricane winds and sending the dega off his back to the floor. The dega jumped to its feet, its long tail grabbing hold of the handrail, and climbed up the side of the train wall, hissing at Chaz, who had pushed Jennifer up against the wall, gun in the air.

"It will be a bloody mess unless you give me what I want. I came for two souls, but I will settle for one," it said, spitting as it spoke and leaping onto Chaz's back.

"You will get no one," Chaz said, spinning the three of them into the subway doors.

"I'll quit, if you give me a deal," the dega said, as it clawed Chaz's face with its long dirty nails. Laughing, it continued, "Blood and disease, on all that you protect." They furiously bounced around the train. As quick as lightning, the dega grabbed two souls, a man and a woman, and spun them around, so that one of the souls was in Jennifer's line of fire. "This one is mine."

"No!" Chaz yelled, "I will give you what you want."

The dega's eyes lit up with fire as it said, "You have the sensibility of a mortal—let us see whether you find the meaning of this season!"

Several shots rang out and Chaz looked around the car to see whether anyone was hit. Everyone seemed okay. Suddenly, as a passenger on the train pulled the emergency cord, the angel Allison appeared and ripped the dega right out of the car by its throat.

Chaz felt the blood run from his mortal body, and he fought hard not to fall. Looking around, he could see vile degas all over the train and in the tunnel, as angels descended on them in a fierce battle. He wanted to move but could not, and, in his last conscious moments, he registered the horrible smell of the degas and the reappearance of Allison with her glorious red robe and light-blue wings. She kept whispering, "Do not forget! Do not forget! It's the child!"

Paramedics worked on his now-human body as police combed the area for evidence and news crews looked for visuals to flash on the six o'clock news. All anyone could report was that this man had jumped in front of the gun to protect the other passengers and knocked the gun from the "crazy woman's" hands. Only one man, whom the police did not take seriously, referred to what happened as a "battle between the angels and demons!" Chaz was rushed to NYU hospital, where, after several hours of surgery, the doctors were able to remove both bullets from his mortal body. Two days later, Chaz awakened, not sure where or who he was but able to feel the pain. Ringing for a nurse, he remembered being on a train and feeling his blood flow out of his body and through his hands. The nurse was able to confirm what he could remember about the accident, but she was unable to tell him much of anything else.

"Where did I come from," he asked her, "and why did that woman shoot me?" There were no answers, only images of a train car filled with frightened people. As the nurse took his vital signs, she told him he had been asleep for two days, and that they had been worried about him.

Seconds later, two doctors entered the room and began to ask him questions, many of which he could not answer. "You had no ID on you when they found you, Mr.—?" The doctor waited for Chaz to finish his name, but he could not.

"Do you remember your name?" the other doctor asked him.

"I know my first name is...Ch..." He had no memory of who he was. The only thing he could recall was a little bit of the action on the train. "Was anyone else hit?" Chaz asked, genuinely concerned.

"No," one of the doctors replied, "but a man was found in a coma from a fall when the train stopped." Chaz sat up in bed, feeling better knowing that no one else had been shot or killed. The two doctors examined him, asking all sorts of questions: "Are you married? Do you have family? Where do you live? Where do you work?" But Chaz could answer none of them. All that he could remember was that he was on a journey of some type, but he could not remember what that was either.

Everyone in the room looked at each other, sure that the journey he spoke of was a direct result of the shock of the incident. They could not, however, fool themselves into thinking that it was physical, since his vital signs and recovery were miraculous. A nurse entered the room. Her ethereal presence made Chaz feel at ease. In her hand was a white envelope, which she handed to Chaz, in front of the doctors. Carefully, he opened the envelope and took out a bankbook. Before opening it, he looked at the nurse questioningly.

She understood his silent question and began to answer it for him. "A man dropped it off at the front desk. He said that he was on the train with you and that you saved his life. I guess he wanted to repay you." Slowly, Chaz opened the book.

"Twenty thousand dollars!" The nurse moved in closer so the doctors could not hear her. "I think you'll need that for your journey, but remember it's only a tool."

"What is a tool?" the younger of the two doctors asked.

The nurse turned and simply stated, "Money." Laughing, the young doctor said, "A very big tool."

Several days later, the hospital ran out of reasons to keep him. Chaz looked at the billfold containing $140 and the identification, which the police said was his. According to the ID in the wallet, Chaz was Harry Miller. As he left the hospital, Chaz could not help but think of the man who had fallen on the train; he had learned that the poor guy was still in a coma.

New York's streets were filled with Christmas decorations. Wow, he thought, the streets looked beautiful and festive. He wished he could remember himself as Harry Miller, but that label did not feel right for him.

Reaching into his pocket, he took out his new bankbook and then his ID, checking the address where he was supposed to live. He hailed a cab, jumped in, and ended up in front of the thirty-story apartment building that Harry Miller called home. He walked into the lobby and checked for his name and the manager's name on the directory.

Chaz knew that he needed the manager to let him into the apartment because he had no key. Strange, he thought quietly to himself, as the manager led him up the elevator and then down the hallway to his apartment. The man did not appear to care for him and was sarcastic when he asked him about being a so-called hero.

When he opened the door and walked into the apartment, Chaz was startled by the starkness of the decor. The living room furniture consisted of a couch, a love seat, and a chair, all protected in plastic. Two lamps sat on end tables, which had to be fifteen years old and were crowded with magazines. A seventeen-inch television set was placed on top of a larger television set, which did not work.

Chaz looked around the apartment, uncomfortable in Harry Miller's apartment. The manager left without coming in but said he would have a key made for him. There was nothing in the kitchen cabinets except for half a bottle of scotch and some mismatched glasses. Inside the refrigerator was more of the same: just a couple of eggs and a can of coffee.

The apartment had two bedrooms. In the one where Harry Miller slept, there were clothes all over the bed and floor. The closet was open, and a coat was hung from the top of the door. Opening the second bedroom's door, Chaz was surprised to see an organized office. It was apparent from the boxes on the floor and the notes on the bulletin board that Harry Miller worked out of his house. Chaz looked at a certificate and degree and realized that Harry Miller was a CPA.

Chaz went through the desk drawers as well as the entire apartment, but the items he found revealed nothing to him, except for one very important item: He was not Harry Miller.

Chaz sat at the office desk, frustrated with his inability to discover anything important. Taking the bankbook from his pocket, he opened it and looked at the initial deposit of twenty thousand dollars. He decided to stay in a hotel room for a few days because the apartment was so depressing.

He noticed that Harry had tacked a strip of paper with a typed-out question onto his bulletin board. It read, "What does Christmas really mean?" Feeling that a curtain had been raised, Chaz took it down from the board and looked at it as he sat at the desk. Instinctively, he knew that this question had something to do with the "journey" the nurse mentioned at the hospital. He was not sure whether it had been the shock or the trauma of the shooting, but he heard an inner voice connect the two items for him. Maybe that was his journey. If he found the meaning of Christmas—if he knew that—maybe he would remember his true self.

Walking through the busy New York streets, Chaz decided that today would be the start of his journey. The first thing on his mind was to find out what Christmas was. The second was to learn more about Harry Miller, the man he was supposed to be. These two questions were the keys to opening the door back to his life.

Chaz stopped a woman on the street and asked her, "What is Christmas?" She stepped away from him like he was a madman, muttering, "Get away from me." Her reaction caught him off guard, and he felt embarrassed, wondering whether Christmas might be a negative thing. I must be more careful, he thought, flagging down a taxicab. When it stopped,

Chaz jumped right in, and the cabby immediately pulled back into the traffic, asking him where he was going. Chaz took a deep breath and tried asking the question again, this time rephrasing it slightly. "What is Christmas, and where can I find it?"

After a moment of laughter, the cabby spoke. "You're not from around here, are you?" He moved across the traffic and turned at the first right. "I'll take you to Christmas."

Chaz sat straight full of excitement. "So Christmas is a place."

"Well," said the cab driver, "not really."

"But you said you were going to take me there," responded Chaz.

Shaking his head, the cabby tried to clarify his earlier response. "It's different things to different people."

Chaz leaned forward. "Isn't there a true meaning?" The cabby pulled to the curb outside Rockefeller Center and pointed to the crowd of people around the giant Christmas tree. "You might find your answer out there."

Standing on the corner, Chaz watched in amazement at the people with shopping bags, some rushing, others sightseeing. He walked around the plaza. Everything was familiar in a distant way, like a forgotten song. While standing in front of the huge tree, Chaz could not help but feel stimulated by its beauty.

A small choir was singing at the side of the tree. Chaz moved closer, standing behind an older woman as the choir began to sing "White Christmas."

He leaned against a wall and glanced at the ice-skaters below. Chaz spoke his thoughts: "White Christmas...dreaming of...so it is a place." Thinking he had been speaking to her, the older woman turned to him and said, "It's referring to snow—you know, snow," she said, looking up into the sky. The blank look in his eyes apparently did not faze her, and she continued. "Snow, it's like rain—an element."

Chaz was confused. "What does that have to do with Christmas?"

"It makes it more beautiful—more traditional. Frankly, I don't want snow, but the kids do. I guess it looks nice the first day and on cards, but…" The woman continued to ramble on about snow, before he politely stopped her.

"I need to know what Christmas is—what it means."

"It's about dinero," interjected a man standing near him. Suddenly, several people joined in to express their different images of Christmas.

"Commerce."

"Family."

"Commercial racket." Finally, a man in a handsome suit took his arm and whispered into his ear, "Walk into the store and watch the money; that is Christmas." Chaz pulled away with fright at the sight of the man's ice-blue eyes flecked with gold. The raised voices from the crowd and choir began making Chaz feel sick and sweaty. It was as if the man's words had poisoned him. He stumbled away into the department store, where the weight of the revolving doors overwhelmed him.

Once inside, Chaz found his senses inundated by the brilliant decorations, rapidly blinking, colored lights, and deafening sounds of cash registers. He wiped his forehead and tried to keep from falling. For a brief moment, Chaz felt an image pass before him, but it happened too quickly to understand exactly what it was. However, the breeze from its beautiful, flapping wings helped him regain his equilibrium. Feeling somewhat better, Chaz continued into the store. Looking up toward the golden ceiling, he spotted the papier-mâché angels carefully placed above the crowd, and felt a sense of hope. Piped-in Christmas music sang of a red-nosed reindeer, which seemed to help put the masses in the mood for shopping. Carefully, he watched as clerks collected money in all forms: checks, credit cards, and cash. Chaz stepped behind a heavyset young woman and asked her whether this was what Christmas was about—spending money.

The woman looked at him as she placed a variety of items on the counter and asked, "What are you, Scrooge?"

"Scrooge?" he asked.

"Look," the woman said, without missing a beat with the salesperson. "I love to shop, but the gifts are to let people know I care."

"Yes, but what is Christmas?"

Paying for her purchases, she kept right on talking. "You want to know that? Go to the third floor. That's the toy department. Ask a child waiting in line to see the fat man in the red suit." "Child?" The child! That meant something, but what? As he enjoyed the ride on the escalator, Chaz thought he heard someone speak to him from behind, but not a soul was there. He read an ad as he passed the women's department on the second floor: "Forget Christmas past, make Christmas present. One she'll never forget." There was a picture of beautiful woman wearing lingerie below the text. Backing down the moving stairs to get a better look at the ad, Chaz startled an older man, who leaned against the railing, afraid Chaz was going to hurt him.

The third floor was decorated to look like a toy land, and in the middle of it all was a fat man in a red suit. Actually, it was an out-of-work actor doing his interpretation. Chaz followed a small boy who was waiting in line to see the man, standing alongside the child as he inched his way along.

"Does this guy in the red suit have the meaning of Christmas?" Chaz asked the boy, as they stopped in line.

"Oh, this isn't the real Santa Claus. The real Santa Claus lives at the North Pole, but he's too busy working for his trip on Christmas Eve to come here. This guy is good for a picture though." A nervous woman moved in on the conversation and Chaz realized she was the little boy's mother.

"Smart kid," he said, just to ease her mind. "I'm out doing a survey on the true meaning of Christmas. Your son here says that Santa lives at the North Pole and that Santa is the true meaning." She was not sure whether Chaz was friend or foe; the world had gotten so crazy. You had to teach your children to be suspicious of everyone.

Leery as she was, she spoke to him. "Well, that he does."

Chaz was not sure what to make of everything because he had heard many interpretations of Christmas in just one day, but he had the feeling he was on to something, and asked, "Where does the real Santa Claus live?"

She answered him without the least bit of hesitation. "The North Pole."

Trying to get to the North Pole was not an easy task, but it could be done. First, you had to fly to Canada, where you had a layover. Then a flight brought you into Greenland and another long layover, and then another flight. Finally, you had to hire a private charter. According to the children, most people would not know how to get to Santa Claus, so you had to be secretive, because Santa did not want to be found. Chaz, however, was well prepared. He had spoken to many children at four different department stores about Santa Claus, and they all knew him.

"Look for Santa Claus Lane," one child said. Another revealed that his workshop would be impossible to find because "it was like the bat cave—hidden."

The pilot flew him around what was known as the North Pole, 150 miles to the north, south, east, and west. Nothing. Jack, the rogue pilot for hire, was a man in his forties with a tremendous amount of mileage on his face and the perpetual smell of alcohol on his breath. "Why don't you tell me what you're looking for, exactly?" Jack said. "Then I can probably help you better."

Chaz looked out the window, feeling a little silly and thinking that maybe the workshop was too hidden to be seen from the sky. "A workshop." Jack looked at him, a cigarette hanging from the side of his mouth. "Whose—Santa's?" he blurted out, laughing, coughing, and spitting out the cigarette as he did so.

"Well, yes," Chaz volunteered, excited about the possibility of Jack knowing where it was located.

Jack became somber with the realization that he might be flying around a crazy man. "You don't look like a wacko."

Surprised by the change in Jack's mood and the tone of his voice, Chaz began telling him about the children and the lady who had told him that Santa Claus was the true meaning of what Christmas was all about.

Jack shook his head and lit another cigarette. "Where the hell are you from, Mars? Santa Claus is a fictional character. Kids don't know any better, and you can't believe most women."

By the time he had brought the plane down, Jack had heard all about Chaz's having been shot. Jack figured it explained why the guy was acting like a loon. As they walked back to Jack's car, he gave Chaz some last-minute pointers. "All Santa Claus represents is the spirit of Christmas—it's all make-believe."

Chaz was devastated. He had found out quite a lot about Christmas from a variety of people, and he was now beginning to believe the voice he kept hearing in his head: "Christmas is just a holiday, like Thanksgiving, only you give gifts." Still, it was confusing. First, someone had told him that Christmas was a place, and then it was commerce, and then people said it was about Santa Claus, who delivered toys. But Chaz had found out that Santa Claus represented only the spirit of Christmas.

Maybe it was just a commercial event, he thought, as the flight attendant placed a glass of orange juice on the tray in front of him. He was going to write all this journey crap off and go back to being a CPA, whatever that entailed. He glanced at the woman who had given him the orange juice and observed her name tag. "Allison, what a pretty name," he said.

"Do not give up. You are on the right track—stay with the spirit." He stared at her lips, knowing that they had not moved. But, surely, she had spoken to him. Looking at him in a peculiar way, Allison said, "It's not the accident that is making you confused." *What?* Chaz thought. Shooting? How did she know? But did she know. And what did she mean by, "Stay with the spirit?"

Getting off the plane, Chaz was immersed in the crowd of holiday travelers. In his heart, he knew that there was a true meaning to Christmas; finding that out was the key to the success of his journey. Intellectually, he understood that most people would interpret many of his actions as those of a crazy person or, as Jack said, "a man who had a near-death experience." Chaz walked through the airport past a variety of concessions, listening to the piped-in Christmas music that was continually interrupted by the PA system and a variety of announcements. A calendar featuring angels was hanging in the window of the gift store, and it drew him inside. As he picked up the calendar and flipped through the photos, the images seemed to resurrect a memory for him. He browsed through the store, finding many artifacts that were angel related, including a soap dish, a candle holder, thoughts of the day, and so on. He could not be sure that what he was feeling was uncommon because he may have seen these types of images all of his life, but something inside of him cried out that they weren't true. Angels. Did Harry Miller believe in angels, and what were these creatures supposed to represent? Chaz wondered whether there was any connection between them and the meaning of Christmas. Or were they simply as fictional as Santa Claus? Quickly, he paid for the calendar and left the shop.

Snowflakes fell past the eleventh-floor hotel window, as Chaz sat in bed, watching them float silently toward the sidewalk below. Sipping his coffee, he felt as if he were trapped inside a recently shaken paperweight, one that caused the illusion of a beautiful snowy landscape.

Something had happened to him, and it was more than the incident on the train. Chaz wondered whether, somewhere along the road, Harry Miller had made a choice, and now, he, as Harry Miller, could not believe that this was his journey. He was a simple CPA with no family, no friends, and no one to love. A life he was not proud of. And so he created this journey that was nothing more than an illusion, just like a snow globe after it has been shaken.

For a brief second, Chaz thought he heard laughter. Now I'm getting paranoid, he thought, finally getting out of bed and walking into the bathroom. Showered and shaved, Chaz dressed slowly, watching a midafternoon news program as he did. He looked out of the window and saw that it was still snowing heavily. Chaz thought briefly of the woman who had explained the meaning of the song, "White Christmas." Suddenly, all of the voices from the past week played in his mind: "It's about money, a time to give, and family."

Finally, the woman on the television broke through the wall of voices filling his head, a welcome relief to Chaz. "And so it's Christmas Eve, and we get ready to welcome the birth of the Christ child."

Everything stood still. Then his emotions went off like fireworks on the Fourth of July. Where had he heard those words? "It's the child. Do not forget!" Chaz finished dressing, grabbed Harry Miller's coat, and left the hotel room for the streets of New York.

The snow was sticking to the street and coming down heavily. Chaz made his way toward TNBS studios. He had to speak to that woman and find out where the Christ child was to be born, feeling sure that would lead him to his journey's end.

He couldn't find a cab. A city bus stopped and Chaz ran to catch it, sliding across the slippery sidewalk into the side of the bus. Inside, the bus was crowded with last-minute shoppers and workers trying to get home. Before Chaz had a chance to take his seat, black smoke drifted from the rear of the bus, blanketing the snowflakes like a bad daydream. The bus came to a grinding halt. The driver frantically began trying to restart the engine as passengers began to complain. After several failed attempts, the bus driver radioed for help and received word that it would take at least an hour or two before another bus with space for passengers could get to them. The passengers headed into the snowstorm, all of them very unhappy with their circumstances. Chaz stood on the side-walk, watching the remaining passengers file out, determined to get to the television studio.

"I'll walk," he said aloud, trying hard to convince himself that he would make it before the newscaster left. The last passenger off the bus was a very pregnant woman with a small suitcase. She was traveling all alone and lost her balance momentarily. Chaz approached and asked whether she was all right. She nodded, holding her gloveless hand up to her face to protect her eyes from the falling snow to see where she was going.

"Are you traveling alone?" Chaz asked her.

"Yes," she replied. She had an eastern European accent. "I go to my sister's, but I don't think I'm going to make it." She gestured to the bus, as if to say, "That is why." He stood looking at her. *Could this be the birth the woman on the news was talking about?* Quickly, he dismissed this thought. The birth must be of a newborn king. Obviously, this woman was not car-rying a king; surely there would be pomp and circumstance if she were.

"Do you need help?" Chaz asked but was relieved when she shook her head. He watched as she walked off, struggling in the snow. Immediately, he felt sure he should not have allowed her to take the journey alone. Halfway up the street, she stopped, dropped her suitcase, and then tried to pick it up. He ran after her, picked up the suitcase, and took her arm. "Please, let me help you. You should not be alone in this weather, especially in your condition. If your baby were this Christ child I heard about on TV, a limo would be taking you to wherever you were going."

The woman's laugh was musical. "Who are you, silly man?" she asked in her broken English. "Do you not know the story of the Christ child?" Before she could continue, she buckled over in pain, and he held her tightly to prevent her from falling.

"Is it time?" Chaz asked. Panic touched his lips as the words passed them. Again, the woman tried to speak but was once more seized with pain. Chaz looked around the empty, snow-blown streets. The woman's face was pale, and fear was in her eyes. "The baby is coming, now! My water break!" Chaz led her to a snow-covered car and leaned her up against it for support. "I'll be right back," he assured her. She grabbed his arm and looked into his eyes. "I'm going to come back; I promise you."

Chaz ran into the street, but there was no one to help. The snow was keeping people inside, and the visibility was so bad that Chaz could not see across the wide avenue. There was a large parking lot on his side of the street, and someone was inside the payment kiosk. Chaz ran to it and banged on the window, scaring the man inside.

"Help me! I have a pregnant woman!" Inside, the man was nervous, thinking that Chaz was trouble. He showed him a gun and told him to get away from the booth. After several attempts to make the man understand without succeeding, Chaz ran back to the woman.

She was holding on to the mirror for support with snowflakes melting on her face. "Just like Mary—no place to have my baby," the woman said, getting weaker with each passing second. He held her underneath her arm for support, and they started walking, with no clear direction.

"Go back to the bus," Chaz heard loud and clear. "What?" he asked.

She looked at him, obviously in pain. "I said nothing." He turned her around and headed back to the bus. They walked a few feet, and her legs buckled.

"Save yourself; forget this woman." Was this the voice of a dega? Dega? Chaz stood upright, looking around him. No one. He took off his coat and laid it on the snow. Then he gently lowered the woman on top of it and began pulling her through the snow, moving much faster than they could walk. In minutes, they were back at the bus, which was still parked, waiting for help.

The snowstorm was now a blizzard, the kind that shuts down cities like New York. Chaz began banging on the door, and the bus driver wiped the glass to see out. As soon as he saw the woman lying on the ground, the driver opened the doors and came out to help Chaz. They placed her on the backseat, trying to make her comfortable.

"Are you all right?" the driver asked her.

"My baby born outside, like Jesus. That's a good sign."

"What is she talking about?" Chaz asked the driver, but he was much too excited to stop and explain.

"You ever deliver a baby before?" Chaz shook his head. The driver ran to the front of the bus and radioed dispatch, who hooked his line into the 911 operators. He relayed instructions from the operator to Chaz, and, together, they delivered a healthy baby girl.

"What will you name her?" the driver asked the woman, as the paramedics finally arrived. "Mary," she answered meekly. Holding on to Chaz's hand, she asked him to come to the hospital with her. He waited with the driver as the medics took her and the baby into a waiting ambulance.

"Yep, we have just witnessed what this season is all about," said the driver.

"Spirit? Like Santa Claus?" asked Chaz, feeling the veil of confusion begin to lift.

"Saint Nick," the driver continued, "represents the spirit of giving. You know, 'God so loved the world that he gave his only begotten son' to save us from our sins. That is why we give gifts because Christ gave the gift of everlasting life."

Looking past the bus driver, Chaz saw a dega, in its horrible form, standing in front of the bus, ready for battle. Degas began surrounding the bus, and Chaz knew who he was again—an angel of the Lord. Like a burst of wind, Allison arrived with an army of angels with the power of a tornado, sending all of the degas out of the bus and into the gutter.

"I must go," Chaz said to the driver. He blessed the man and stepped off of the bus and back into his wings. Flying alongside the ambulance, he watched as it drove to the emergency area of the same hospital he had been taken as a human. Chaz knew he had another soul to protect: the new baby, Mary.

Watching as the nurse carefully laid the baby into the cradle, he flapped his wings behind her. At this age, a child can still see angels, and Chaz was easy for her to see above the nurse. She cooed enthusiastically. "Oh, you are a friendly one," the nurse said, responding to her burst of affection. Chaz moved on to the room with the man who had been hurt during the train shootout. He came out of his coma and told the doctors he was Harry Miller. He also told them that while he was in a coma, he dreamed about an angel who was looking for Christmas.

"Did he find it?" a doctor asked.

"Yeah, I think that's why I'm talking to you now."

Chaz walked through the hospital corridors, flapping his wings. He passed many angels who were soldiers of God in the battle against evil. The bells from the churches sang out their song, letting the city of New York know that it was Christmas. In the midst of the holiday season's joy, celebrations, and despair are angels reaching out to help and protect all of you. So the next time you have an unexplained incident or feel comfort from a stranger who suddenly disappears, remember: There are angels in your midst.

The End

Lost in Florida at Christmas

Lord, help me to realize how brief my time on earth will be.
Help me to know that I am here for but a moment more.

PSALMS 39:4

"Jingle Bells" playing over the pool speakers seemed out of place in the eighty-degree heat. My brother and I dived into the pool and tried hard to suppress any sad memories we might be having. The multicolored Christmas lights, blinking on and off around the pool, deadened the Christmas spirit for these two New York boys—which was exactly what my father had hoped the trip to Florida might accomplish.

My mother had died two days before Christmas the previous year, and we were doing our best to avoid the first full Christmas season without her. Sitting on the edge of the pool, I let the sun dry me off. It felt good on my face. It was Christmas in Fort Lauderdale and the first time we had been out of the New York/New Jersey area in our entire lives.

I have to tell you: if you've never experienced Christmas outside of a cold climate, walking past Christmas trees and decorations in shorts and no shirt is a very strange experience, especially the first time.

Because we lived in the north, Florida had always seemed exotic. And the place where we were staying, the Polynesian Village, added to that impression. Palm trees adorned with Christmas lights surrounded the pool, and small bamboo huts offered drinks, towels, and sunscreen. Tropical flowers, bushes, trees, and the strong sunshine further enhanced the exotic feel. Inside, the hotel workers were dressed in Hawaiian shirts and dresses. A large fishpond in the small lobby contained large tropical fish. By contrast, the dark restaurant was lined with bamboo booths.

My brother, two sisters, and I were sharing a room. Mike was nineteen at the time, I was seventeen, and my sisters were ten and fifteen. Our twenty-one-year-old brother was spending Christmas in New Orleans, so he was not with us. We moved in quickly and emptied our suitcases, packed too full of clothing we would never wear.

We had an additional travel companion—my father's partner in crime, Daniel Cody. At the time, we thought the two men's antics and sometimes-illegal behavior were cool. My brother and I were trying hard to convince ourselves that we were budding gangsters and that Daniel and my father could teach us the ropes. In actuality, they were nothing more than grifters, as lost as the kids they were supposed to be chaperoning.

Mike, who was as tough as nails when it came to fighting, was one of the most sensitive people I have ever known, but he spent his life trying hard to hide that vulnerability from the outside world. As his younger brother, though, I was not a threat. I do not think he felt the need to hide these emotions from me.

Anyway, we were in Florida, attempting to pretend that we were just a family on vacation and not the lost souls we had been feeling like for the past year. Although I didn't understand it at the time, we were in the process of changing our orbits. If you remove the sun, the planets will spiral out of control into darkness. We didn't yet realize that our mother had been our sun, and that our family was beginning a journey into darkness. Florida at Christmastime was intended to slow our spiral.

Mike and I were planning to follow in our father's and Daniel's footsteps. We dressed sharp, had attitudes, and thought we were extremely attractive to women.

We talked about making scores that would put more money in our pockets: Phony credit cards, pyramid schemes, and stolen art work—these were some of the possibilities. But we had no idea how to actually carry them out. Execution was not important, though. The possibility of adventure—the thought of what might come—was the real goal, even if it was only in our minds. Our plans for the first night were to use our fake IDs to get into one of the fancy disco clubs lining the beach and canals. Music from the Bee Gees was all over the radio, and we did our best to look like John Travolta from *Saturday Night Fever* before leaving the hotel for the night spots.

The night started perfectly well. The fake IDs were working, and every place we hit allowed us in. As "Staying Alive" played, we laughed and goofed around, acting more like the teenagers we were than the slick young men we were trying to impersonate. We danced with older women and drank screwdrivers, impressed with the size of the clubs. The Elbow Room had one large bar on the patio that overlooked a swimming pool and the beach.

After several drinks and a few dances, we sat at the edge of the crowded bar, surprised that none of these people had to go home. After all, it was Christmas Eve. Our conversation switched from chasing women to our opinions of what each member of the family was going through. You can run from some things in your life, but no matter how hard you try, you cannot run from yourself or where you come from. Deep in our souls, we were our mother's sons. The seed of faith that she planted when we were little boys would always help to create the best in us. It would be our strongest asset, and although it would take years and many painful journeys to realize this truth, our faith would always be the home we went back to find.

We each ordered another drink and became silly with good humor as we listened to Thelma Houston singing, "Don't Leave Me This Way." We went back and forth between laughing and having fun and wondering whether coming to Florida had been a good choice. We knew that the hotel room had no Christmas decorations and that our younger sisters would not have any gifts to open on Christmas morning. Even though they knew that before we came to Florida—the vacation itself was supposed to be the gift—Mike and I could not help but feel that they would be disappointed.

The music and noise in the bar seemed to disappear as memories of that final afternoon in December muffled all the sounds around us. Life had not been the same for the twelve months since Mom died, and we did not anticipate getting back to any kind of normalcy anytime soon.

It was December 23, on a very cold winter afternoon, when we drove across the Red Bank Bridge that took us to Riverview Hospital, where our mother was losing her battle with cancer. Mike and I had gone out earlier in the day to buy our mom a gold cross. She had wanted it for the last four Christmases but never got it. In retrospect, I guess buying a gift for a dying woman was an odd thing to do. But when you're among the living, you never quite accept that a person is going to die, no matter how much time you spend by his or her deathbed. In some primal way, I think people need to be able to please the dying person or, at the very least, to send them off with some last act of love because they cannot save them. After a year and a half of feeling helpless, this was a small way of fighting back. By the time we arrived in her room, our mother was struggling for her last breath.

Here, on this night in Florida, we all remembered things about those last minutes differently. Mike remembered that my dad, my uncle, and I had been standing around the bed afraid to do anything. He didn't remember me getting really upset and leaving the room, or my dad coming out to comfort me. He thought we were all at her bedside when she died.

But I remembered feeling guilty because I had been so overwhelmed that I started to sob and crawled out of the room. My dad came out and walked me around the hall. We were about to head back to the room when I heard a commotion because Mike kicked out the glass where the fire extinguisher was kept. It was at that moment I knew my mom had passed away. We both remembered standing outside my mother's hospital room, my dad, Mike, and I, and just holding on to each other and crying. Neither one of us remembered much after that.

The bartender yelled, "last call," and we decided we didn't need any more to drink. Outside, the warm Florida air was in total contrast to that stark December afternoon now haunting us. A key piece to the puzzle of our lives had been removed, and we would spend the next ten years trying to replace it with alcohol, drugs, violence, and other bad choices. We walked along the canal, thinking about the last months of our mother's life. The memories were right there at our fingertips, like a photo album ready to open. Little by little, we turned the pages to relieve the pain—and maybe exorcise a few demons. We talked of how wonderful Christmas had always been in our house. No matter what the circumstances, our mother could always pull things magically out of her sleeve to make the season special. We now realized that Christmas would represent a dichotomy for us from this point forward. Somehow we would have to make a choice—would Christmas represent sadness and death, or would be able to tap into the joy of the season and the love we once shared as a family during this season? Knowing this, we tiptoed into the past, choosing the Christmases filled with joy and happiness—avoiding the last Christmas that changed it all.

"Remember the year we got the pool table, or the year it snowed, and we really had a white Christmas?"

"How about the first year in the house? All of us sitting around the fireplace singing Christmas Carols, drinking hot chocolate."

We walked for a block in silence, both of us thinking about our own times with her, both fighting tears, each trying to be strong for the other. But the road to this Christmas led us back to last December, with its bare trees, hard ground, and cold air. Florida could not prevent the inevitable: we were going back to a room without a sign of the current Christmas season, filled instead with only the pain of Christmas past.

The pharmacy on the corner sold everything you can imagine: groceries, bath products, perfume, and candy. As we stood outside the front door, Mike decided that we should spend our remaining money on Christmas presents for our little sisters. There was no argument from me.

Inside, the place felt surreal. Elevator Christmas music was piped in over speakers, and the only other customers at two in the morning on Christmas Eve were insomniacs and other lost souls. Mike and I walked around the store picking up bath gel, candy, curling irons, cheap perfume, and wrapping paper. We spent all the money we had saved for Florida.

Back at the hotel, we asked the clerk whether we could borrow some tinsel and ornaments from the tree in the lobby. When we told him about our sisters upstairs, he said, "Take what you want." We joked about dragging the entire Christmas tree into the elevator and upstairs to the room but thought better of it. In the morning, the girls woke up to wrapped presents, surrounded by tinsel and candy. We laughed long and hard at some of the presents we had come up with. In the end, we realized that Christmas is really about the people you love. What is important is sharing it, not the quality of the presents. Give me the ten people I love the most in the world, and keep the presents.

As the years moved on, Mike and I often discussed how the road can make you stumble and how, if you get the chance, you need to set things straight. Mike is gone now, and like most of us, he did his share of falling.

But in the end, he became a good man, struggling to do what was right. I guess that night was a moment in the journey, when we were temporarily lost in Florida at Christmas.

Eventually, we would find our way home.

The End